I0573417

INFINITE INDIES 2022

ISBN: 978-1-64456-546-9 [Hardcover]
ISBN: 978-1-64456-547-6 [Paperback]
ISBN: 978-1-64456-548-3 [Mobi]
ISBN: 978-1-64456-549-0 [ePub]

Library of Congress Control Number: 2022947199

INDIES UNITED PUBLISHING HOUSE, LLC
P.O. BOX 3071
QUINCY, IL 62305-3071
www.indiesunited.net

Dedicated to every person who ever took a
chance on an unknown author.
Thank you.

Table of Contents

Foreword

by Lisa Orban

From a young age I developed a passion for books. They became my escape when times were hard, a shield in awkward social situations, they filled the lonely hours with new friends, and, always, it was a joy to fall into a new world far from where I lived. In distant lands found between the pages of a book, I grew up.

But, it was in anthologies I found true delight, dropping into multiple worlds, in many different voices, that all called me to join them in their adventures – all in one book! Ever on the hunt for new authors, I couldn't resist any new anthology coming out, particularly in the SciFi and fantasy genre. They introduced me to previously unknown authors, and encouraged me to seek out more books by any who caught my fancy. Some I may have never have given a chance without the brief interlude of a their short stories to explore more of their works.

In the days before the internet, this was sometimes the only way to find a new author without becoming overwhelmed at the number of offerings stacked endlessly on the shelves of a library or bookstore. Hundreds of books all vying for your attention without a guide to take you by the hand and lead you to the promised land where you can completely lose yourself. But anthologies bypass that decision fatigue, each story is just a short investment of your time, and if you don't like it, nothing is lost as you only need to turn the page to find a new story waiting for you.

When I opened Indies United, remembering my love for anthologies, I offered our authors the chance to collaborate on one, and for three years now, we have presented a new Infinite Indies in November. A fun meet & greet between pages, and a chance to explore the writing styles of many of our authors all at once. I hope as you read these stories you will find a new author, or more, that you want to take a chance on and get to know their books better. Each story is as unique as the writer that created them, and who knows, you may find your next great book love somewhere within these pages.

Happy Reading!
Lisa Orban

INDIES UNITED PUBISHING HOUSE
PRESENTS

Infinite Indies 2022

A MULTI-AUTHOR ANTHOLOGY

INDIES UNITED PUBLISHING HOUSE, LLC

A Walk in the Woods

Ketan Desai

Whose woods these are I'm sure I know.
It belongs to the local borough;
Who won't care if I stop here
And watch the verdant woods, bright and aglow.

My little dog must think it queer
To stop without a tree stump near
By the shimmering, sylvan lake
The longest day of the year

He gives an impatient whine
To ask if we can stop wasting time.
The only other sound's the cry
Of a solitary Eagle in the sky

The woods are lovely, bright and upsweep,
And I have no promises to keep,
No attachments or desires over which to weep,
No miles to go before I sleep.

Beat

• ● ⬤ ● •

by Jake Cavanah

Curtis Groffle had left the office disgruntled about having been assigned work that kept him there until the bell. He had been doing it for so long he could work quickly and had, just barely, enough respect to forgo the pleasantry that was staying at his desk until 5:00 p.m. Unless some "additional, last-minute" responsibilities came his way.

This is what he chose to complain to himself about during the first two beers of the night. Then, he knew, as the beers kept coming, so would his past.

Curtis spun his longneck Rolling Rock around on the coaster between each sip. Here in the depths of The Brown Room, his drink of choice was considered middle of the road. Not that great, but also not too shitty, but, then again, there was no such thing as "too shitty" at The Brown Room.

With about a quarter left in his second bottle, Curtis signaled to Amy he was ready for another. He downed what remained to make room, and she leaned over the bar to swap out the empty one for its replacement, getting out of the way just before he belched.

Curtis took another lengthy pull and set it on the bar top harder than he meant to, startling the patrons a few stools away from him. Who he failed to notice.

The third beer was when the memories of the last thirty years kicked in, starting back when he had had so much promise.

The beautiful wife.

A new house.

Prosperous company.

Thick, healthy hair.

In good shape.

Oh, how things had taken a turn.

The company experienced a down year when their sons were four and six, and every decision Curtis made after that only made things worse.

More debt.

Customers leaving for the competition.

More angry banks.

Investors pulling out.

Not qualified to refinance.

Expensive bar tabs.

Good employees leaving.

His affair.

Forgetting about his sons' baseball games.

Forgetting about his sons.

Katherine's suicide.

Curtis used to think about ending the clusterfuck that was his life, but he was far too cowardly.

His sons were forced to take care of the only parent they had left at very young ages. They did what they could to help their father, but, as they quickly learned, you can only do so much for someone who doesn't want to be there. They had begged Curtis' parents, siblings, old business partners, and anyone who would listen to help save him, but the response was, regretfully, "Sorry, there's nothing we can do."

Curtis remembered his sons first approaching him with a heavy heart, but when they were teenagers and had had enough, it was their anger he remembered. They would verbally abuse him when he stumbled home at all hours of the day and night. His eldest would try to teach him a lesson by leaving Curtis bloody and bruised on the front porch, but he would just wake up and do it all over again.

Then came the accusations about their mother's suicide being his fault, which became more frequent the more they learned about his downfall.

Curtis never admitted it, but he blamed himself, too.

Like clockwork, a man wearing a hat low over his face took a seat in the corner of the bar. He was there every evening, and Curtis had never seen him order more than one Rolling Rock. On account of both being regulars with the same drink preference, Curtis would often nod his way and lift his glass to him. The man would nod back, and that would be it.

Curtis had almost mustered up the courage to approach him a couple of times before deeming it useless.

Close to ten beers in, Curtis closed out his tab and told Amy bye. The man's go-to booth was on the way out, and when Curtis passed by the man said, "When are you going to stop playing with fire?"

"Excuse me?" Curtis said.

"You drink a twelve pack every night and drive out of here. How long do you expect to keep getting away with that?"

"Hopefully not much longer."

The man shook his head and muttered something under his breath.

"Cheers," Curtis said.

The man said nothing.

Curtis had been gone for about ten minutes when the man received a text message.

How is he tonight?

The man responded, Same old dad. I finally

said something to him.

Did he recognize you?

What do you think?

Just give up man. He's not worth it.

The man typed out and erased multiple messages before sending back, I wish I could.

His older brother had been begging him to let their dad go for years, but if he truly didn't care, he wouldn't be so curious.

Spare

●　●　⬤　●　•

by Eirynne J Gallagher

"All right," she said. "That really isn't necessary."

She stared at the large, unmarked pistol. Judging from the rough-milled edges someone had assembled it from spare parts. Officially, the only weapons on Luna were carried by Security and the Navy, but Earth hadn't shipped seventy-five thousand morons to the moon. Engineers, craftsmen, architects, mechanics, electricians… no one got off Earth without a valuable skill, which meant that no one got off Earth without knowing things. Knowledge is either good or ill, and generally it ended up both.

The huge, dirty hand clutching the gun had scars and scabs. It led to a slab-like arm, hugely muscled and smudged with dirt and grease. A loader's arm. The dark eyes that stared at her over the barrel of the gun were blank and merciless. She smiled sweetly.

"Really," she said soothingly, "that isn't necessary. I'm just looking for my fiancé. If you haven't seen him, that's the way it is. I'll be on my merry-"

"Shut up," the gunman said.

"Okay," she said, "but this really isn't a big deal. You don't have to make it a big deal."

He snarled at her. "You just shut up. Wait here. Wait and shut up."

Sometimes they weren't all geniuses. Someone had to empty the garbage and shift cargo. Maybe he was native, but he didn't look like it. Natural-born Loonies usually had far less mass, having grown up in low gravity. Luna held some two million people now. Most of them were honest, hard-working people. Some were shifty. Some were downright bad. Same as everywhere, really.

Elise held still. The guy looked unstable and she had no desire to get shot. She glanced around. The small shop had emptied out when she showed the photograph around. No one knew him. No one had seen him before, ever. Despite the lack of interest in her photograph and her questions, the owner had somehow signaled the big guy. Elise assumed she'd done something to anger the big guy because he'd pulled the gun and sent his companion, a dirty-looking whip of a kid who reminded Elise of some kind of a snake, bounding for the door. The kid, now, *he* was native. He had that narrow, strip-jerky look to him that the natural-born got no matter how many calcium pills they ate and no matter how much time they put in at the public gyms.

The walls of the tiny shop bulged with random equipment. She could see from where she stood a set of gloves from an EVA suit, cans of dried cheese, a fishing net, rolls of the ever-present Velcro strips, and the internal boards from what looked like a targeting computer from a Navy frigate. She wasn't surprised. These low-town shops carried whatever they thought they could make a profit from, and few things were as profitable as salvage. Everyone on Luna had to become a jack-of-all-trades, fixing their own plumbing, their own computers, and their own gear.

Elise heard a noise in the back of the shop, and the snake-like kid bounced in. Her host didn't turn.

"Well?" he asked the kid. "What did they say?"

"The Man says bring her, Gus," the kid said in rush of words. "The Man says he wants to meet her."

"You heard him," Gus told Elise. "The Man wants you. Move."

Elise hesitated. He pointed with the gun. They floated through the doorway to the back room. In a dead-end storage room a floor-to-ceiling shelving unit had been dragged aside. Behind it set into the wall of the city, stood an airlock door.

Elise eyed her captors. They pointed. Elise spun the wheel and opened the door. Stale but breathable air expelled.

She looked at Gus again, who stabbed at the door with the gun. Once she floated through it the gunman came behind her. The kid followed, his greasy black hair streaming as he dove head-first, balling up at the tail-end of each bounce step and springing forward again. The big guy closed and dogged the door. She spun the wheel on the second door and opened it.

Elise stopped in the narrow corridor and waited. Gus pointed left, she went left. She bounded down the alley with giant-steps. Gus and his pal floated only a couple of feet behind her.

At the crossroad at the end of the tunnel Gus said, "Right."

The corridor narrowed at the far end and in the dingy light she could see a door set in the stone. She stopped in front of it, wondering if Gus were smarter than he looked.

Yes he was. He stopped five feet from her and let his sidekick float up. He waited until Elise scrunched up against the wall before pounding on the door. After a moment a bolt shunted out of the way and the door opened a crack. A face appeared and looked the kid up and down. The door opened wider.

"What you want, Gob?" The voice from behind the door grated like rough stones underfoot.

"The Man," Gob said, "he asked for us."

A wheeze of a laugh. "The Man don't ask. He tells."

"He told us come. You gonna open up, or what?" the little snake, Gob, asked.

From behind the door came a grunt and the door opened wide. Gus motioned with his gun. Gob went first, Elise followed. They were in a narrow access tunnel. It looked like one of the original maintenance tunnels, from when Luna was first settled.

Luna City is a giant corkscrew into the meat of the moon. The city's design had large platters of living and working space stacked on one another and they narrowed as they sank into the rock. A stone wall two feet thick hugged the top, bottom, and outside of each platter. The walls looked like old-fashioned concrete but had been designed in a lab. Stone still made up the lion's share of the composition, but it contained a slurry of other chemicals designed to bond and flex, to keep atmosphere in, and harmful things out. It wouldn't leech, it didn't break down, and it would last forever unless you nuked it, a lot.

In order to lay the foundations of humanity's second home, tunnels had been blasted into the bones of the moon. Forms had been erected to hold the miracle mixture of rock and chemicals that would make life on Luna possible. Elise realized that she and her sketchy new companions were *outside* the walls now. She had left Luna city. She swallowed hard.

They followed the gentle curve of the corridor. They passed two airlocks. At the third one, Gus told her to stop. He pounded on the door.

In the lock stood a woman with a cap of messy blonde hair in a crisp, clean shipsuit. She stepped aside for them. Gus made Elise go first. When he floated in from behind, he pinched the woman on the cheek. She flinched and pulled away and Gus laughed at her.

The lock cycled and the inner door opened into some kind of storage bay. Sealed crates along the walls bore unusual, hand-painted markings. Gus shoved her toward the doorway. She drifted into a large, open room, bare walls, no chairs. She floated to the center of the room and turned around. Gus parked himself at the door and watched her.

After what seemed like an eternity, Gus moved aside and another man bounded into the room.

His eyes were bright green like jade glass, restless, and his square jaw jutted like a shelf. He floated to a standstill with his hands in his pockets and examined her carefully.

She looked back, blinking frequently in involuntary response because he didn't seem to. Her eyes watered just looking into his.

"Who are you?" he asked. His voice, pleasantly even, rumbled low his chest.

"My name's Jenny," Elise said. "Jenny Carter."

"So what, Jenny Carter?"

"I don't know," she said. "I'm not sure what's going on."

"You've been flashing a picture around, bugging everyone on the level. What do you want?"

"Who are you?" she asked him.

"Why do you care?"

"Because if I'm being held like this, guys with guns, secret rooms, then I'm getting somewhere. So who are you? And do you know where this man is?" She held out a picture, an id photo of a man with a bare skull and bright blue eyes. Her mystery man glanced at it.

"Why are you looking for him?"

"Does it matter? I need to find him. Do you know him?"

The man shook his head. "Nope."

"Bull," she said.

His eyebrows shot up. "Bull?"

"You're lying to me," she told him. "I can tell."

"How?"

"Because you kidnapped me." She held out the photo again. "Where is he?"

"Why do you care?"

"That's my business," she said.

"Now it's mine. Tell me," the man said.

"No," she replied.

The man actually smiled. "No?"

"You heard me." Elise crossed her arms in front of her and glared at the man. He grinned.

"Lady, you have some brass, I'll give you that. Why are you looking for him?"

"Who are you?" Elise demanded again.

"I'm the Man," he said. "That's all you need to know."

"Okay, *The Man*, where is he?"

He sighed. He took his time answering. Finally, he said, "You can call me Chapp."

She nodded. "Well, Chapp, he's my fiancé and he's missing. I'm looking for him."

"Fiancé, huh?"

"Yes. He even gave me this ring," she said, holding out her hand. Chapp took it. He examined the small gold band. Inset on the band there appeared to be a ruby. He looked closer and realized it was a plain rock. A red rock.

"What the hell is this?"

"It's a Marsrock," she said. "He brought it back after his first job, mining on Mars. He proposed to me the second he had the ring made. It's just a piece of common igneous basalt rock. No real value. But it's from Mars, and he dug it up with his own two hands, and it's mine, and I'm going to be his wife."

Chapp looked her up and down. "He had good taste."

14

"Thank you. Now where is he?"

"What's his name?" Chapp asked.

"Jeremy," she said. "Jeremy Horvath."

"Well, Jenny Carter, I haven't seen your beau. Are you sure he's missing? Maybe he just ran off with someone else. Ever think of that?" Chapp laughed.

"He wouldn't do that," she told him. "He loves me. And I love him. And I'm going to find him."

"I'm sure he's around," Chapp told her. "Now get lost."

"No."

"No?" Chapp looked blank. "No?"

Before Elise could react he had her by the front of her suit. He lifted her off the ground. She didn't look impressed and she didn't struggle. In the light gravity of Luna City, she weighed about twenty, maybe twenty-five pounds. She stared calmly down at him.

"You don't tell me no," Chapp said. "You don't want to tell me no."

"I don't care what you say. Do you think I'm scared of you? I told you no and I meant it. You know something and you're holding out on me. I'm not leaving until you tell me where he is."

Chapp half-smiled. "You have brass, all right."

He dropped her. She bounced gently on the balls of her feet. Chapp opened his mouth to say something, but a small commotion behind them made him stop and turn. In the doorway, the little one, Gob, whispered to the big one, Gus. Chapp stared irritably at them.

"What is it? I'm in the middle of a conversation."

Gus waved him over. Chapp said, "Sorry. It'll be just a second."

"Don't worry," she said with a sour look. "You can take your time coming back and trying to intimidate me. I'm not going anywhere."

Chapp grinned and floated over to the door. They whispered to one another. Chapp looked over his shoulder at Elise. She waved.

Chapp looked back at Gus. "You're sure?"

"Sure, I'm sure. You know we always double-check this kind of thing. Our guy in the office said it."

"All right. Good work. You shot him her pic, right?" Chapp said.

"Soon as she started nosing around, boss, you know that. She isn't Security," Gus said. "Our guy says no. But that pic..."

"What about it?" Chapp said. Gus showed him a readout.

"All right. Good work." Chapp floated back to Elise, one long lazy bound.

"Where were we?" She asked him.

"We had just reached the part where I threaten to toss you out a lock without a suit if you don't start being straight with me," Chapp said, "because you're full of it, lady."

"I don't know what your problem is, but I'm telling you-"

"Who's Randall Carter?"

Elise stopped short. She looked shifty for a moment and sighed. She closed her eyes.

"I don't know what you're talking about," she said. "I've never heard of any-"

"Now who's being insincere?" Chapp asked. "You know why I'm asking."

"No," Elise said, staring at the floor. "I don't."

"Look at you. You can't even look me in the eye. So, you don't know what's what? Then tell me, Miss Carter... Who's Security Technician Randall Carter? Because the name on his ID says 'Jeremy Horvath.'" Chapp said.

Elise made a show of grinding her teeth and balling her fists. She looked away; at the wall, at the floor, anywhere but Chapp's smiling, triumphant face. Finally she said, "Randall is my brother."

Chapp nodded. "There," he said. "Doesn't it feel good to tell the truth?"

"Bite me," she said sullenly.

"Manners, Miss Carter," Chapp said. "Be nice to me."

"I don't see why I should," she said, "you lied to me. You obviously know where Jeremy... where Randall is."

"Well, it's an imperfect world," Chapp said, "but like I said, he's around. Why are you so hot to find him? I mean, he's not a nice guy. He's an undercover Security narc. That's not the most noble of professions."

"He's a good man," Elise said, "and he does a job no one wants to do. Someone has to keep order."

"There's keeping order," Chapp replied, "and there's keeping legitimate businessmen like myself from being able to turn a decent profit and support our families."

"Are you married?" she asked.

"Oh, hell no," Chapp said. "What woman would put up with *me*? And even if I found one that would, who would marry a woman like that? No, I'm more of a... well... a free agent."

"How nice for you," Elise said. "But we're getting off the subject."

"No, it's related. Because all of a sudden, you're not about to be married. All of a sudden you're someone's unmarried sister. And you happen to be just my type," Chapp said.

"No," she said. "I'm not your type. I only date humans."

Chapp's bright green eyes narrowed. "Cute."

"I try," Elise said.

"You know," Chap said slowly, "a thought occurs. You come in here saying you're engaged to be married to a man who turns out to be an undercover agent for System Security. You're aware of his cover identity *and* his real name. So maybe, just maybe, you're not some worried sister at all. Maybe you're a colleague."

"What?"

"Maybe you're a Security agent too," Chapp said. "No matter *what* my guy says."

"I promise you," Elise said with sincerity, "that I am *not* a Security agent."

"That sounded good, what you just said. I believed it. But I don't. Take off your clothes," he said.

"Excuse me?" Elise asked.

"You heard me. Strip. I bet you're wired. You'll do it, or my guys will-"

Elise tugged the zipper down the front of her suit. She shrugged the material off her shoulders. She untabbed her boots and stepped out of them and tugged the suit off her legs. She stood up straight.

"Now what, genius?" she asked Chapp. She had the momentary pleasure of seeing him caught completely off guard.

He took a second to gather himself. He pointed. "Gob, take her clothes and destroy them. They could be monitored."

The smaller man darted forward and grabbed the suit and boots. He took a long, lingering look at Elise, who didn't react. Gob started to turn away, and stopped.

"Boss," he said in his lisping manner.

"What is it, Gob?" Chapp stared into Elise's eyes. "I told you what to do."

"Yes, Boss," Gob said, "but there's something on her leg."

Chapp looked down. Elise looked away.

"Turn around, Miss Carter," Chapp said in a frigid voice. She turned. His eyes dropped to her right hip and thigh. A foot-long scar, angry, red, bumpy, stretched the length of her thigh.

Chapp whistled. Something had torn the large muscle on the woman's thigh to the bone. In the gravity of Earth, she'd never walk again without a serious limp or a cane. And the healing? Six months, maybe more. Chapp bet it hurt every day. Elise's arm twitched. She hadn't covered her body in modesty when she stripped but Chapp knew her hand wanted to cover the ugly wound in her leg.

"What happened?" he asked.

She looked away. "I was a prospector. It was a mining drill. Went right through the ceramic hull of the digging machine. Went through my suit, into my leg. I had to sit with the drill in my thigh for two hours before they could get to me. The drill kept my suit integrity."

"You're a lucky woman."

"Yeah," she said. "I'm lucky. I wake up screaming sometimes because I'm so lucky. There's still pieces of ceramics in there, despite three surgeries, because I'm so lucky. Not magnetic, don't show up on x-rays. They move. It hurts."

Chapp nodded. "Sounds like a burden. Well, Miss Carter, like I said, your brother's not here. So if you-"

He stopped. His lips stretched in a slow, slow smile that didn't radiate any kind of happiness that Elise had ever heard of. Her skin crawled watching that smile.

"What?" she asked.

"He's your brother?" Chapp asked. "He's your *brother*?"

"Yes," Elise said. She eyed him warily. "What of it?"

"Gus?"

"Boss?"

"Take us below," Chapp said. "Take us down. I want to see the doc."

"Yes, sir," Gus said. "You want me to scrounge up some clothes?"

"Did my order include a contingency for clothing?"

"Uh, no sir. Sorry, sir." Gus sounded chagrined. "Right this way."

Gus went to the wall and pressed a circuit board against it. Lines formed and a panel opened. Chapp gestured in a grotesque parody of gallantry. Elise smirked at him and bounced into the small cube. Chapp followed and Gus came last. It was crowded and Elise couldn't help but press against Chapp. It was either that or Gus, and if she had to choose, it wouldn't be Gus.

Chapp, to his credit, didn't press his advantage. He could have, but he didn't. She didn't trust his altruism but that didn't mean she didn't appreciate his restraint. She was pleased, however, that the Jenny Carter ID had been convincing thus far.

The walls of the elevator were rough-pressed handmade steel. Chapp and his people inhabited the outside of Lunar society in a literal sense. They weren't just leeching off the remnants of Luna City but adding their own touches, like the rooms, like the elevator. Who knew what else they'd built? She stood with her hands clasped, fiddling with her ring.

"Nervous, pet?" Chapp said. "Don't worry. There's no need to worry."

Elise looked up at him. "Do you believe that?"

"Of course I believe it," Chapp said. He grinned at her and said, "You don't believe me?"

"I wouldn't believe you if you told me you were talking," she said.

Chapp laughed.

"Where are we going?" Elise asked him, remembering to put a quaver in her voice.

"Down to my office," Chapp said. "Down where I do business and make a living."

"Let me guess, you sell ice cubes to Eskimos

and ovens to people in hell." Elise said.

"Oh, no," Chapp said. "I sell water to drowning victims, and rope to men about to be hanged."

Elise let out a grudging laugh. Chapp smiled at her. "Glad to know you're not afraid."

"Are you kidding? You're so terrifying that the only reason I haven't wet myself is because I haven't had anything to drink in a couple of hours. I'm dehydrated."

Chapp smirked. "You don't hold yourself like a terrified woman. You're acting like you're in charge of everything."

"Well, I came looking for Randall and everyone told me they hadn't seen him, including you. Then you tell me you have no idea where he is. *Then* you tell me his real name. You could have just killed me and yet here I am. Tell me, who's in charge of whom?" Elise said. "Because I have to tell you, from where I'm standing-"

"You mean in your skin, in a box with bad men?" Chapp said.

She smiled and inclined her head. They stood in silence for the rest of the descent. The elevator jerked to a halt. The doors opened and Chapp stepped out. Gus gestured and Elise hopped out of the elevator. She followed Chapp down another narrow passage into a medical bay. Equipment filled the room, but only the center. Along the walls were stacked more of the cargo containers, each with a hand-painted mark on it.

She glided to a halt. Chapp turned around. "What's the matter, cupcake? Out of pithy comments? No bravado?"

"W-what's this?" Elise asked. She eyed the machinery. "What is all this?"

"This? This is my business office. Welcome to it." Chapp said. He waved over a man in white scrubs.

"What's cooking, Boss?"

"Run a baseline on her. I want a full spectrum. Everything. Put a rush on it, okay?" Chapp said. "This is top. I don't care what else you've got brewing. Put it on simmer or throw it out and start new. Get me?"

"Got you, Boss." The white coat turned and grabbed a couple of instruments out of an autoclave. He approached Elise. She drew back. She bumped into Gus and stopped.

"What the hell, Chapp? What is this?" she said.

"This?" he replied. "This is just business, sweetheart. Don't sweat it."

He turned away. She heard him mutter as he left, "Sister."

"What about it?" she said.

He turned. The gleam in his eye was unmistakable.

"What about it?" she demanded.

"You're his sister? No kidding?"

Elise ground her teeth and made herself look

petulant. She extemporized, "Twin. So what?"

Chapp smiled widely. "Twin sister. That's good. That's outstanding. That means you're a genetic match to him. Did you know your brother has a rare blood type? Of course you do. Because you have the same blood, right?"

She could answer only because she had studied Randall Carter's bio. "Yeah. AB, RH negative. Why?"

The doctor smiled warmly and pointed to the nearest bed. If he seemed surprised at the sudden appearance of a naked woman in his medical bay, he didn't show it.

"I need blood, and saliva, and some marrow," he said. "The marrow's going to hurt. Brace yourself."

"No way I'm letting some would-be veterinarian stick me," Elise said. "Thanks but no thanks. I'm leaving-"

Gus grabbed her upper arm in one meaty fist. She looked down at it and back up at him. He weighed more than twice what she did and his arms bulged with muscles. She stood there naked and defenseless and silently counted the ways she could cripple or kill him with just her left hand. She held her reactions in check and glowered while Gus guided her to the bed. She sat.

"My name's Hanson," the tech said. "I'll make it all quick, okay?"

"I don't like needles," Elise told him.

"Who does?" Hanson said. He rubbed her arm with a swab and slid the needle home. He drew out two ampoules of blood and set them aside. He taped a ball of cotton to her arm. He took a sterile swab on a stick and held it up. "Give me a nice, wide smile."

Elise opened her mouth and let Hanson swab the inside of her cheek. He put it the swab in the container and sealed it. He put all of the samples on a tray, pushed it away, and said "Roll over on your stomach."

"Why? You can type from blood and saliva both. Why do you need my marrow?" She struggled, but Gus pushed her back. She rolled over. "Why are you doing this?"

Hanson swabbed the iliac crest, the knob of hip bone closest to the surface. He picked up a tiny needle and injected Elise with a numbing agent. Her leg felt suddenly like a block of wood.

"We're going to run a cancer and disease screen as well, just to make sure you're healthy," Hanson said. He picked up a large-bore needle.

"You might want to look away," he said.

"I've seen worse," Elise told him. He looked at her scar.

"Looks like," he said. And he set the coring needle against her skin. She closed her eyes and thought about all the ways she could kill the doctor using the coring needle and while she daydreamed she played with the red ring on her finger.

Soon enough the doctor finished his ministrations and slapped a bandage over the seeping hole. She winced when she stepped off the gurney.

Hanson took her samples and walked to a bank of machines. He began preparing the samples for examination. Chapp gestured to Elise.

"Let's go."

"Go where?"

"Someplace we can talk," he said. "I've got something I want to tell you."

The bare walls were rough stone and more of the storage containers lined them.

"Did you just move in or something? What's with all the boxes?" she asked Chapp. He pointed to a couch. He poured himself a drink and fixed one for her. Like most Luna glasses, these balloons had almost-enclosed tops to keep liquid in during sudden movements. They always reminded Elise of pitcher plants back on Earth, carnivorous plants that killed their prey by trapping them inside their bell-like bodies. They made her skin crawl. He handed her the bulb. She sipped. She looked at the glass.

"Bourbon," he said, "from Earth. Nothing but the best."

"For you?"

He smiled. "No, pet. For you. Think of it as a last meal."

She looked at the glass again.

"Could I get a straw? I'd like to make it last."

Chapp laughed. "Can't say you're not a cool one under pressure."

"Well, you become a fatalist when you spend enough time working the rock," she said. "Miners don't have a good chance of retiring."

"That's true. How long have you been a miner?" Chapp asked.

"Four years," Elise said. It was somewhat true. Her first job on Luna after leaving the Navy had been in the mines. She knew enough to talk the talk. "Four long, dangerous, dirty years."

Chapp nodded. "Your brother?"

Elise's face closed down. "My brother is a different story."

"Tell me."

"No," Elise said.

"Excuse me?" Chapp said. "I didn't quite hear you. I didn't hear you because no one tells me no. Ever."

"You've said that before but it's an inaccurate statement," she said, "because I just did. Again."

He frowned.

"I don't care. You think I'm an idiot? You didn't bring me here to show me my brother and let us be off on our merry way. And I'm not sure what the deal is with the medical procedures, but that can't bode well for me. So don't threaten me, Chapp. Everything you've done so far has been a loud and clear message. You don't intend me to leave this place. So drop the rough-and-angry act. Just tell me where my damned brother is, you twerp." Elise sat back and sipped her bourbon.

Chapp laughed out loud. "You *are* a cool one. You know, if I didn't know better, I'd think I might have a chance with you. And I'd want one. You're something else."

"Oh, yeah," she said. "I'm one of a kind. Except that I'm not."

"Right, yeah, because of your twin brother. Hey, is it true that twins can often sense when the other one's in trouble?" Chapp asked.

"I don't know about all that, but when Security told me that my brother left in the middle of a shift and didn't come back, I knew something was wrong. They told me to drop it, in a not-so-subtle way. In a way that told me I should let it go, head back to my cube and wait for the inevitable commendation letter and a handshake from some appeasement engineer in a pretty uniform to tell me how brave and honorable my brother was. I'm going to settle for that? I don't think so," Elise said. "So I took his junior partner out for some drinks and managed to wheedle the name Randall worked the streets under out of him. I took a picture and combed the levels. I started at the bottom of the city and worked my way up on the assumption that he'd probably be in the dirty parts rather than the clean. And I started to get some glints in the eyes of the street people. So I redoubled my efforts. Then that shop-keep up top shined me on while he called your boy Gus. I knew I'd struck a rich vein."

Chapp nodded. "You're persistent, I'll give you that. I got news of your unsubtle questions two days before Gus got the call. I got curious. I'm the one sent them, Gus and Gob. My people have strict instructions on what to do about cops and other sight-seers, but you caught my eye, looking for your brother like that. I wouldn't have remembered him but the name you used, that stuck out in my memory. And I was impressed with your moxy. Never taking no for an answer. So I sent Gus up to arrange a meeting. And here we are."

"Here we are," Elise agreed. She sipped her bourbon and crossed her legs. Chapp's eyes darted to her naked body and back to her eyes. She smiled a little. "Some first date."

"Don't expect an encore," he said. "I'm not that kind of guy."

"You're a peach," Elise said.

"Well, you may or may not think so in a little while." Chapp got up. He paused at the door. "I want you to know that no matter what happens, I told you the absolute truth. Your brother *is* around." He looked over at Gus. "She stays here."

30

"You got it, Boss," Gus told him, and posted himself in the doorway after Chapp floated out. Elise stayed where she was, coolly sipping the last of her bourbon.

"Does 'she stays here' mean the room? Or the couch? Because I'm dry," she said, holding up the empty balloon. Gus didn't speak.

"You're charming," she said. She stood up, keeping her eye on him. He didn't move when she floated over to the bottles. She carefully poured herself a new drink. She could feel Gus's eyes on her backside. She turned to him and smiled when his eyes snapped up to her face. He blushed slightly.

"Don't worry about it," she told him. She settled herself back on the couch. "If it bothered me, being naked, I wouldn't have made it off Earth. You know what it's like. You spend almost a month naked anyhow, going through the medicals."

Gus didn't nod, but she though she saw his eyes agree with her, if that was possible. She finished the second drink. Gus suddenly moved aside, and Chapp came back into the room. He looked at Gus.

"Go find Gob, would you?" The big man nodded.

Chapp looked at Elise. He held up a piece of paper. His face was red.

"Guess what?" he said.

"I don't know," she replied. "Could it be… that he wasn't my brother at all?"

She and Chapp stared at each other.

He smiled. "You got it in one. So, you're not related to Randall Carter at all. Who are you?"

"The question is, who are *you*?" Elise asked. "I've never heard of you, or even rumors about this place. How long has this place been here?"

"Yeah. I'll tell you that. Like hell. Security doesn't know where we are, and they're not *going* to-"

Elise fiddled with her ring again. Chapp looked at her with narrowed eyes. He looked at the ring. He looked her in the face.

"You bitch," he said disgustedly.

"Language," she told him.

"You're with Security. I *knew* it," Chapp said. "I knew it. Always trust my instincts. I'm out of my mind. I must be out of my mind."

"Possibly. And I told you: I'm not with Security. I'm an outside contractor. But there's hope," Elise said. "Give me Carter and we'll talk. Otherwise it's not going to go so well for you."

Chapp smiled. "You know, you're good, cookie. But you're not that good."

"He says, knowing that his whole operation is blown," Elise mocked him.

Chapp frowned. "That may be. But it's

nothing to me. I'll just start up somewhere else. If you'll excuse me."

"Sorry, *Boss*, but I'm going to have to go ahead and disagree with you. You're not going anywhere." Elise moved between him and the door.

"Honey, I continue to appreciate your enthusiasm and confidence, but if you don't move I'm going to break your neck with my bare hands," Chapp said, moving toward her. She stood her ground.

"Where's Carter?"

Chapp stopped.

"Tell me," Elise said. "Where's Carter?"

Chapp smiled. Then he guffawed and began laughing. "Oh my God... I can't believe you. You people are idiots. Seriously? You have *no* idea, do you?" He pointed at her leg. "You think you're the only person maimed on the job up here? You think you're the only one who got screwed? Look at your leg, genius. How's your breathing? You were a miner. You know how dangerous the dust is. And that's just on equipment. That dust gets everywhere. It's like ground glass in machines. It kills a suit in, what? Three trips? Four? Gets in the folds of the cloth. In the joints. Ever see a slow leak caused by dust?"

Elise nodded. "Comes with the territory."

"Oh yeah? Every hear of a slow leak in a Security suit? Or Navy?" Chapp said.

Elise said nothing.

"And that's just the equipment. Let's talk human costs. Silicosis, asthma, lung cancer... Black Lung died out in the early nineteenth century on Earth. But how many miners did you know needed lung transplants up here? How about cancer from inadequate solar shields? Micrometeorites? People are dropping like flies. They get maimed. They get sick. They need help."

"And you do... what? Sell insurance?" Elise asked him.

Chapp pointed to the crates stacked along the walls. "Nope. We deal in those."

Elise didn't look away from him; she wasn't green. Chapp kicked back away from the door into the room. "Go ahead."

Elise eyed him. She moved to the first crate. She broke the seal on the box and opened the lid. She looked into the crate. She looked at Chapp again and back into the crate. She closed the lid and resealed it.

"That was... that was a lung," she said. "Was that a lung?"

"You got it, sweetheart. I told you the first time you asked... Carter? He's around. He's in half a dozen people by now. High demand, that rare blood." Chapp said with a smile. "The machine breaks down, you get replacement parts to keep it going. What happens when people break down? What do *they* do?"

"You're proud of yourself? You're... you're stripping people down for parts, and you have the gall to act... what? Magnanimous? So you provide your service for free?" Elise asked.

"Of course not. I'm not running a charity. But what are you going to do? I have expenses. At least there's an option. Go to Security with your problems, what do you get? Or the Navy? The medical supplies go largely to them. Not the average Loony. I mean... you know what? I'm done arguing with you. Now, if you'll excuse me," Chapp made to head out the door.

"No," she said. "I don't think so."

"I'm losing my sense of humor about you, sweetheart. Move."

"No," she said.

"Move," Chapp said. "*Now.*"

"No," she said. She stood loosely on the balls of her feet with her arms at her sides. He grinned.

He flexed his hands, ready to reach out and grab Elise by the throat. She decided to let him. She took a deep, deep breath. Those hands closed around her neck. He lifted her off the ground. She dangled from his hands with her arms still at her sides. The angry mask of rage twisting Chapp's face changed suddenly. He looked surprised. The grip on her throat slackened and she floated to the ground while Chapp looked down.

The scar on Elise's right leg lay open, the latex falling away from the perfect skin under it. Her fist clutched the stiletto formed from ceramic hull material as it slipped from his side. She held it up.

"I told you there were still pieces of ceramics in there," Elise said. Clutching his stomach, Chapp sank to his knees. He stared up at her.

"You... you're supposed to a-arrest me," he said. "You... you can't..."

"Let me stop you right there. Randall Carter? No, he wasn't my brother. And no, he wasn't my fiancé either. But you know what? I *did* start out as a miner. And when that drill pierced my cab, missing me but holing my suit? Want to take a guess who kept me alive? If Randall hadn't been there, I wouldn't be *here*," Elise told him. She looked at the knife in her hand. "It's about the only thing that could get me to agree to this stupid assignment anyway. And *you* parted him out like a broken-down driller."

She examined Chapp, whose eyes were bright with hatred.

"You're not dead yet?"

Chapp snarled at her. "Going to be a while with a gut wound, you stupid-"

"No," she said with a cold smile. She raised the stiletto. "It really won't."

She zipped the front of the new shipsuit to the

neck. She rolled her shoulders to settle it on her body.

Lieutenant Hartnell didn't look away while she dressed, for which she respected him slightly more. He wasn't insincere.

"We're still mapping the tunnels but there's practically a whole city under here we never suspected. We've been pouring troops in. The… uh… the victims… well, it's going take months to identify them all. But the disappearances should stop, at least for a while. This is a huge market. We don't expect it to dry up completely."

"Nor should you," Elise said, "but get on top of it, Hartnell. This is horrible. Life up here's bad enough."

She threw the stiletto underhand. Throwing a knife well in low gravity takes skill and Elise practiced. The knife stuck into the hand-painted symbol on one of the crates.

"Make sure I get the bonus as well as the agreed-upon price," Elise said. "I had to put in overtime on this one."

"You're all heart," Hartnell said. "You belong here."

At his joke they looked at the crates. Elise looked at Hartnell.

"You're a jerk."

"Yeah," he sighed. "I know. I'll have the paymaster authorize the transfer. And thanks for this, Rosemonde. I know you didn't want to-"

"Drop it," she said. She stopped at the door. She turned to Hartnell. "Look… Carter… he was married, right?"

Hartnell nodded. "Yeah. I've got to go see her soon."

"Give her my check when you go," Elise said.

"Aw. That's-"

Elise put a hand on the knife. Hartnell shut up. "No problem," he said, swallowing hard.

"Good," she said. She headed for the door.

"Hey," Hartnell said. "Elise?"

She stopped. "What?"

"Where's Chapp?" Hartnell asked. "Where's the mystery honcho we heard so much about?"

Elise turned. She looked down at the dagger. She tugged it out of the crate. She studied the blade for a moment, looked at Hartnell and smiled.

"He's around," she said.

The End

Granpa Rides with Santa Claus

• • ● • •

by D. Krauss

"Granpa, do you believe in Santa Claus?"

"Absolutely."

"But," Oscar spluttered, "Billy and Jesus said there is no Santa Claus and you're a baby and stupid if you believe it."

"So I'm a baby and stupid?"

"Well." Oscar became flustered. "No!"

"This Billy and 'Hay Suess,'" Granpa kept rocking but put the book down and peered at Oscar, "tell me how, in a mere seven or eight years of life, they've managed to develop such amazing powers of deduction and analysis."

"Huh?"

"Never mind. How do they know?"

"Their parents told them."

"Hmm. What did your Mom and Dad say?"

Oscar dithered, looking at the floor, "Well, nothing, really."

"Tell me their response and be accurate."

Dang it. Granpa was on him again: be precise, be accurate, always accurate. He hated this. "They both just kinda laughed, said Billy and Jesus didn't know what they were talking about. But Mom said I shouldn't believe in fairy tales."

"She did, did she? Idiot," Granpa muttered under his breath but meant for Oscar to hear. Oscar shifted uncomfortably. "So you think Santa Claus is a fairy tale?"

"Isn't he?"

"Answer the question. Don't respond with a question."

"You do."

"I'm Socrates, I'm allowed to."

"Huh?"

"Don't say 'huh?'!"

"What?"

"Better. So, you *do* think Santa's a fairy tale? And after he brought you those Harry Potter dolls last Christmas."

"Action figures, Granpa."

"Whatever. And after I helped get those down the chimney."

"Granpa."

"And that's a tight fit, too."

"Granpa, c'mon!" and Oscar threw his hands out, frustrated. What was it with grown-ups? They treat you like a baby and make up stupid baby stories and grin at you like they said something brilliant. Man! "Just tell me, Granpa."

"I'm telling you! Every Christmas, me and Nick zip around the world, sharing a bottle and having a good ole time. Although," Granpa made a rueful move at his lower back, "those rides are getting harder on me."

Oscar made a sound of disgust and turned to leave. "I'll prove it," Granpa said to his back.

Oscar was wary. "How?"

"Christmas is what … three days from now?"

"Two, Granpa."

"Not that you're counting or anything, right, boyo? Here's what I'll do." He leaned forward, a glint in his eyes and a conspiratorial smile on his face. "It'll drive your parents crazy. I'll leave two things, one magical, one impossible. How's that?"

"Huh?"

"Don't say … oh never mind. How does that sound?"

Oscar set his face. "Granpa, you're crazy." Just crazy. Like Mom and Dad said when they didn't think Oscar was listening, dementia and delusions and nursing homes and becoming too hard for us to handle may be a nurse. Whispered conversations in doorways and stairways and bathrooms after Granpa had done something heinous (Oscar liked that word), caning the dog or soiling his pants or throwing something at Dad.

"As a loon, boy!" Granpa barked and threw his head back and his face was glowing and wild and became centuries while storms of death raced across his brow and the lost souls of hell beamed from his eyes, yet another light, peaceful and pure, flowed there, too. Oscar was terrified and relieved, tossed on currents he could not see, helpless, shriven, ripped and tortured, cradled and loved.

"Granpa," he breathed, frozen.

"Oh, sorry." Granpa was Granpa again, settling back absently into the afghan. "I forget myself sometimes. I'm old, you know. Be three hundred next May."

Oscar ran.

*

Christmas Eve dinner. Oscar squirmed against the collar and put a surreptitious finger under his tie to loosen it. So this is what hanging felt like.

"Stop fidgeting," Mom said to him as she passed with a plate of yams. Yuck.

She set them on the white tablecloth next to a big bowl of mashed potatoes flanked by another bowl of creamed onions, a big basket of rolls, and green bean casserole, escorts to the platter of browned, steaming roast begging to be carved. Other bowls extended down the table: cranberry sauce and gravies and corn and more rolls and even a dish of deviled eggs. Candles fluttered and red cloth napkins, folded to look like roses, bracketed the gold Christmas dishes, each printed with a different holiday scene. Oscar studied his— a smiling Santa, dressed in what looked like red thermals, dancing some kind of insane jig, beard wagging and eyes twinkling while an elf and a reindeer looked on with astonishment. Just them. No Granpa.

"This is all mine, twerp," a petulant voice snarled and a too-pointy elbow jammed too hard in Oscar's ribs. Cousin Harold. The evil one.

"Ouch!" Oscar said and glowered at Harold, who hunched over the deviled eggs with a predatory look. Yeah, like fatso needed those.

"What are you boys doing?" Aunt Rachel frowned through her pointy glasses at them, looking so much like a crow that Oscar had an urge to caw.

"Oscar's trying to take them all," Harold said.

"No, I'm not!" he glared at Harold, who grinned evilly. "Oscar!" Aunt Rachel's spine-breaking frequency kicked in. "You'll have to share."

"Jerk," Oscar muttered to Harold.

"Dweeb," and they were off, a small shoving match under the table, of which Oscar was getting the worst.

"Knock it off, you two," Dad smacked the back of their heads as he walked by.

"Ow! I didn't do anything! Oscar was doing it!" and Dad and Aunt Rachel were yelling at Oscar and then at Harold and then at each other and then Mom came in with her, "What's going on now?" voice and Oscar sat back, shaking his head.

Jeez. Every year.

"All right!" a basso interruption, almost feeling like Dad's thwack on the head, and they all stopped, surprised. Granpa sat at the top of the table dressed in a white tux shirt with a red bow tie and suspenders, face flushed, rheumy blue eyes on fire. His mouth was a crimson line through the beard and, for half a second, Oscar swore he *was* Santa Claus.

"Little more of the Christmas spirit, I think." Granpa rumbled.

"You don't have to yell, Dad," Oscar's Dad said while he moved with murderous purpose towards the roast, carving knife in hand.

"I didn't yell. Besides, how can I hear anything over you idiots? Sounds more like New Year's than Christmas." Granpa puffed out his cheeks.

"Idiots?" Aunt Rachel gasped in genuine horror and Mom railed at Granpa over his choice of words and Dad clacked the platter with the knife to regain order while Harold took that opportunity to throw another elbow into Oscar's side. Oscar grimaced.

"Tonight, boy" whispered in his ear and Oscar whipped his head around but no one was there. Astonished, he stared at Granpa, who regarded Aunt Rachel like a cockroach while, at the same time, turned his head and giving him a wink, but, that's impossible; he was facing Rachel while commenting on her's and Mom's substandard ancestry, using Harold as proof, while Oscar was proof of Dad's and, consequently Granpa's, superior genes. Something like that. Oscar rubbed his eyes. What had he just seen?

Another round of horrified protest from Aunt Rachel who couldn't understand why her sister allowed her father-in-law to say such terrible things about their family when they had so many good members like Mom and Dad and their two brothers who were CPAs and doing very well thankyouverymuch and if there was any group of people with broken chromosomes ... well. So Mom had to fight Rachel because it was a slam on her choice of men and Dad looked to Heaven and loudly prayed for divine intervention and Harold surreptitiously gobbled eggs. Oscar elbowed him hard in the ribs, pleased with Harold's sudden eye bulge and doubling over.

"All RIGHT!" It felt like a fist in their collective guts and all of them lost their breath, not just Harold. Everyone stared at Granpa. Dad was blown back a bit and his face went dark. "Don't do that stuff, Dad," he said with the voice usually reserved for Oscar's math tests.

"What?" Granpa was innocent, eyebrows raised and hands out in supplication but there was a mischievous grin on his face. They all looked at each other, not sure what happened, frowned at Granpa, not sure what he'd done. Granpa winked at Oscar again.

"You know?" Oscar whispered to Dad.

Dad looked down at him and there was Granpa on his face, younger and re-sculpted, but him just the same. No, wait, not really, something was missing. Dad turned silently back to the roast. Oscar blinked. He'd had a revelation, but about what, he had no idea.

*

Midnight. Oscar shivered in the dark hallway. It should be Halloween, he thought. You're not supposed to be scared on Christmas Eve.

That he was standing in shadow and gloom made it scarier. He should run for the Christmas tree and its twinkling top star imbued with the power of mangers and angels and shepherds on high, ward against evil. But he'd get no answers there, so he was here, beyond protection, where everything dark and evil breathed. Baby Jesus wouldn't like that; it crossed some kind of line. He could almost see Jesus' frown.

Don't abandon me, Oscar thought.

He stood outside Granpa's door. Mom and Dad's bedroom was two doors away, separated by the master bath, but might as well be across the country. If Oscar needed to escape, he couldn't go to them. What would he say, that demons rushed out of Granpa's room with the hellglow on their faces, seeking his soul? Right. He'd have to flee upstairs and the safety of blankets and sheets, his fleet of model warplanes flying cover from their strings overhead while scattered plastic soldiers formed patrols on the floor, Harry and Dumbledore closing ranks on his desk. He'd be safe. He should go now. But you have to face the dragon, or the dragon comes for you.

He touched the doorknob and felt a coldness in it that was almost alive. He gasped, pulling his hand back quickly, but the spark of it stayed on his fingers, flowing around his hand and stabbing up his arm, questing, curious, snuffling toward his chest. It was the cold of forlorn hope, of lost things, and he couldn't breathe from the sheer terror of it. It swirled about and then touched down through his breastbone, surrounding his heart. He was seized, helpless, the prisoner of grief and the cold thing sought the warmth in him, absorbing it, digesting everything alive. Oscar felt his blood shrivel and all the joy of being a kid, soccer games and crazy running and going down slides headfirst and jumping off swings, dissolve.

But then it stopped, snuffled with some surprise, actually sent him a brief greeting, zipped down his arm, and leaped across to the doorknob, gone.

It took an effort to regain breath. A wind blew in Granpa's room and something walked about the floor unhappy and the cold thing crawled across the walls. Granpa was not there. But his servants were.

Oscar fled to his room and his own servants.

*

"Oscar?"

The dragon.

Oscar whimpered and burrowed deeper into the blankets. Become a small target, let the airplanes and Harry and the soldiers delay the bite and fire of the scaled thing lorded over his bed...

"Oscar!"

Not a dragon; Mom. Or could dragons imitate people? Cautiously, he edged one eye out.

Looked like Mom. "What are you doing, Oscar?" Sounded like her, too.

"Hmh?"

"It's Christmas morning. You usually beat us downstairs by three or four hours. What's wrong? Are you sick?"

Oscar popped awake and sat up, throwing the blankets off, and looking about wildly. Cold Christmasy sunlight filtered through pristine snow and pure, iced air streamed through the window. This was a Holy Day. Inviolate. No dragons.

"Oscar?" Mom looked at him with true concern.

"Ah! Mom, no I'm fine, I'm okay." He paused to get a breath and verify that nothing dark lurked by a bedpost or peered out of a closet. They can't, he chided himself, this is Jesus' birthday.

He looked at Mom and felt warm and safe, like something had been beaten back. "Mom," he whispered.

"Oscar, you're starting to scare me."

"Sorry, Mom, I'm all right. I just had very weird dreams. They seemed real." They were, but Oscar wasn't about to tell her that.

"Oh, honey," and she was all Mom, sitting on the bed and smoothing back his hair, her brows wrinkled with Mom concern and eyes wide to detect hurt. "I'm so sorry" —like dreams were her fault— "maybe you ate too much at dinner and Granpa was so loud and mean ..."

Granpa.

"Is he here?" Oscar asked quickly.

Mom patted his shoulder gently. "Well, yes, Oscar, he is, but you know he'd never hurt you and doesn't really mean anything with his yelling ..."

"No, no." Oscar shook his head, "I know that. Have you seen him?"

"You mean this morning? Oscar, it's still pretty early." She gestured at his big Spiderman clock, which read 7:30 in red digital script.

"Can we go see?"

"Go see what? Granpa?"

He nodded eagerly. Please, Mom, please, let's open the door because the cold thing and the unhappy thing have fled before Christmas' Power and Granpa should be there, soot covered and smoky, a bit of reindeer hair drifting about him, and then Oscar would know for sure.

She gave her half-note laugh, "Oh no, Oscar, no way. Granpa's a bear enough when he sleeps regular. Do you think I'm going to poke the beast?" and she smiled and poked him gently in the ribs.

He twisted away, irritated. "C'mon, Mom, we don't have to wake him, just open the door. I want to see him."

She stared. "Why do you want to do that?"

Because, Mom, something Deathless and World Shattering lived in the old, fat, stooped body of Granpa. It was not Granpa. It may never have been Granpa. Don't you see?

"Just do," he muttered.

"Oscar," the exasperated voice and the throwing of hands upwards, "you have been just the strangest boy this past week. I'd think you'd want to see what's under the tree before anything."

He blinked. Well, yeah, when you think about it, he did. I mean, hey, it's Christmas.

It's Christmas, you idiot! Get moving!

"Yay!" he leaped out of bed with springiness only possible in eight-year-old boys, startling Mom, who jerked back to avoid the damage eight-year-old knees and elbows inflicted. Oscar bounced into the hallway and pounded down the stairs, Mom's "Oscar!" only impetus and he grabslung around the banister, sliding the last few feet into the den on his knees.

The golden glow of morning framed and rayed the still lit tree, a roil of colored and natural light, and all of it said Peace and Joy and Good, everything Good. There is nothing cold and unhappy here. A bubbling flew up Oscar's stomach and he gave himself a hug, laughing out loud.

Dad was standing next to the tree, surprise stamping his face. "Well," he asked, "'bout time. Aren't you going to open your presents?"

*

Oscar sat back, content. He was half buried in wrapping paper and bows and boxes and loot, scattered and torn like the evidence of a passing tornado. What a haul. A *Battleship* board game, cool. Pads and helmet for street hockey, very cool. A Playstation with five games, three of which Mom won't let him play. Absolutely the coolest. He graciously accepted the socks, the sweater, the knit cap and the chess set, in the light of all this coolness.

Mom stood near the fireplace holding a gown against herself, looking long and hard down its length to check its fit. Dad stood opposite, satisfied, arms folded, watching. "You always know what I want," she purred, "it's like magic."

Magic.

Oscar chilled. His eyes widened and he peered hard at the paper-and-ribbon junkyard. Lots of stuff under there: clothes, mostly, and Dad-presents like fishing tackle, a timing light (whatever that was), some slippers … wait. There, at the back of the tree, barely noticeable, camouflaged by the trash.

A box. No, two boxes.

The chill turned blizzard because Oscar swore he'd plowed that area at least seventeen times in his brutal search for presents and they'd simply not been there. He'd have noticed them right away because they weren't even presents, they were wooden and plain, no wrapping on them.

"What's this?" Dad said and Oscar watched in horror as Dad pulled out the two boxes, his grunt and effort marking them as heavy.

"What's what?" Mom looked over from the wall mirror.

Dad flourished the two boxes before stacking them on the couch, "These. They're not marked."

"Really?" Mom frowned and stood next to Dad, staring down at them. "Funny," she said, "I don't remember seeing those."

"Me neither," Dad agreed and joined her in contemplation. "Well," he said suddenly, "let's open them."

"No!" Oscar couldn't help it. They both looked at him, surprised, but he didn't care. Put the boxes back, Dad. Better yet, throw them in the fireplace. Because, when you open them, the world will change. Forever.

"Oscar!" Mom tutted, "they're not yours, at least they're not tagged as yours. Don't be so selfish," and she laughed and reached down and pulled at a little recess on the top box. The lid slid open.

"What on earth?" Mom stared inside. Dad's brow furrowed. Oscar held his breath, not daring to move because he knew it was the dragon, small and desiccated but, in the next moment, sprung to full life and they'd be eaten; or it was the cold thing, or the unhappy one, and they'd be ice and misery, forever. Mom pulled out a bunch of straw and an object.

Oscar blinked. A doll, a wooden painted doll of a woman wearing a scarf around her head.

"A matryoshka!" Mom squealed and rapidly brushed away the remaining straw. "Oh, you rascal!" She exulted at Dad. "Where'd you find this?"

"I didn't, I swear." Dad placed a hand on heart as proof but Mom wasn't listening, she was busy turning the doll's middle. Oscar watched the doll come apart in her hand, revealing a smaller doll inside.

"See, Oscar?" Mom held it up. "This is called a nesting doll. Each one's got a smaller one inside, all the way down. It's from Russia. I've always liked them but good ones are hard to find and, well, this is a good one!" Mom was quite thrilled and Oscar's fear subsided. Okay, so maybe Dad had pulled a fast one.

"Hmph." Dad turned to the second box. "Well, let's see what this is," and he slid it open as the protest rose to Oscar's lips then died because, well, the first one had just been a doll so, what could be so bad?

"My," Dad breathed.

Mom was too busy with her new family of shrinking dolls to look, so Oscar moved where he could peer over Dad's shoulder. A book, purplish grainy leather binding with a thick red cord woven through it, filled just about the whole inside. *The Moderne Taeles of Faerie*, was printed across the face in a gold script Oscar should've had a rough time deciphering, but didn't. A plate of thin beaten metal with a swirl of color on it lay right above the title. As Oscar watched, the color formed into a unicorn standing in front of a forest. "My," Dad said again and gently pulled it out, setting it reverently on his lap.

"George," Mom whispered Dad's name with an urgency that made them both look. Mom was holding the last tiny doll upside down, staring at the bottom of it, her face white.

"Mary?" Dad was alarmed and moved towards her in a spasm of protection. Oscar's chill was now permanent.

"George," Mom looked him full in the face, "this is a Mamontov."

"What?" Dad did not understand.

"A Mamontov, George. One of the very first matryoshkas ever made. This is museum quality. Priceless. Where did you get it?"

"I'm telling you, Mary, I didn't get it. I have no idea where it came from."

Mom stared at him a moment and then was back on the doll, "This is impossible."

Oscar gasped. He took a step back, watching Mom's stunned, enraptured face. No.

Something nudged him. He looked down to see the book pressed into his ribs. Dad was holding it, staring at Oscar with an unreadable face, maybe sad, maybe afraid, he wasn't sure. "This is yours," Dad whispered.

Oscar looked down at the plate. The unicorn swirled into view, tossed its head and silver gleams flew from its eyes and became stars that rolled about its diamond hoofs then rose to make a canopy under which elves sang and fairies danced and gnomes looked furtively out of shadows and there was a glade of oaks, the men there cloaked and bearded and a thousand years in their eyes, the moon on their heads and they all turned and looked at him.

Magic.

Oscar took the book and gently placed it under his arm. Dad regarded Oscar for a full moment with a face of such loss, then attended to Mom, who was going to faint any moment now.

Oscar slipped away.

*

"Granpa?" Oscar whispered.

It was day outside but not in here, where shadows lived and stalked each other and avoided the pools of light which stalked the shadows and danced something ancient around Granpa's bed, hiding him then showing him, each passing of the light a different aspect. There was old Granpa, jolly and teasing, then dark Granpa, death incarnate, then young Granpa who had walked with Merlin and ridden the eagles and gave Tolkien his history. Then just Granpa.

"How do you like your gift?" Granpa's voice from the depths of the blankets, a whisper of bone dust, feathers across stone.

Oscar took a fearful step back, "I…"

"S'all right." There was a shuffling deep in his bed and the shadows and their light adversaries gathered about. Granpa sat up and blinked a few times and one of the shadows rubbed against his cheek. He brushed it away absently and Oscar watched as it fell among its brothers, all reverently touching where Granpa had touched. Oscar shivered. Not fear. Thrill.

"Santa says 'hello,'" Granpa said as he fumbled around his shirt, "aah," pulled out a pipe, said a word, and it flared. He drew in smoke, "Don't tell your Mom," he winked.

Oscar could only stare.

"Wild ride." Granpa shook his head. "I swear he gets crazier every year. You know, this time, he buzzed a Russian air patrol? Nuts. He's going to get a missile up his ass, one day."

Oscar giggled.

"Don't laugh," Granpa said sternly, "you'll probably be with him when that happens. And don't tell your Mom I said 'ass,' either."

"I'll be with him?"

"Sure!" Granpa scrutinized the pipe. "Toldja I'm getting too old for this crap. But you'll have to do a lot of studying first." Granpa pointed at the book.

"This?" Oscar looked down at it. "It's just stories."

"Oh, it's much more than stories, much more," Granpa chuckled, "but I think you know that. Tell ya what," he bounced up, scattering the shadows and light, "why don't you take the book outside and read the first story. Let me sleep a bit more."

"But Granpa, it's snowy."

Granpa smiled. "You really think that matters?" and Oscar felt something stir within, a sense that he stood apart from cold and wind and rain, commanded it, actually.

"You go on now. I'll be along later. Meet you in the glade," and he fell heavy against the pillow.

Oscar watched him for a moment with the outside pulling at his shirttail, come out, play with us, these games embrace horizons, these friends companion gods. Come out. He shivered, delighted again.

"Oh," Granpa's voice rumbled from deep within the blankets, "one other thing. Go easy on your Dad. It skips a generation." The lights gave way to the shadows and here, in the middle of morning, it was the middle of night.

Oscar walked slowly out of the room, clutching the book to his chest. It clamored at him to hurry and things pushed at the binding but he told them to calm down and they grumbled but stilled. He slipped out the back door, his bare feet gliding over the snow, not cold nor wet, a hawthorn tree calling to him. He sat on a proffered branch and was gently lifted up, hidden from view. Mom wouldn't remember him for a few hours, assured by something that he was all right. Dad would worry but would say nothing. It was out of his hands now.

He opened the book. And soared.

Grief

by Michael Deeze

The room felt small and cramped, insufficient to hold the tidal emotions that were swirling within. It was too warm, the air too humid. Sweat had collected in my crotch and armpits, and caused my ass to stick to my underwear when I would pace the room. It had come to this. This crossroad of grief, despair and finality. It had been a long journey to this point, a hard slog. There had been no highs. Only lows. The certainty, the inevitability tragic but expected. Hope a fools wish only. This time to fight no more, to recognize the futility and not waste energy that could be put to better use.

It was fitting that the sun, beyond the window glass, had hidden behind a thick overcast. Even it recognized the somber occasion and masked its brilliance in reverence. The lights of room, similarly dim, setting the mood. I turned the page and read on.

"She weeps over Rahoon, this one is

by James Joyce.
Rain on Rahoon falls softly, softly falling,
Where my dark lover lies.
Sad is his voice that calls me, sadly calling,
At grey moonrise.
Love, hear thou
How soft, how sad his voice is ever calling,
Ever unanswered, and the dark rain falling,
Then as now.
Dark too our hearts, O love, shall lie and cold
As his sad heart has lain
Under the moon grey nettles, the black mould
And muttering rain."

"How sad." The voice whispered. "Such despair."

"Really, I thought it was beautiful. We always remember our first real love, don't we?"

"Read another." The whisper seemed urgent. "Please?"

Clusters of interventions hung from the scaffolds of health all around her. Their sheer numbers testament to the expense of survival. Each with its unique 'ping', or 'beep'. In the corner, the ever-present white hospital dwarf gasped each breath as the chest of the shrunken angel above rose and fell in unison.

"Are you sure? You seem tired today."

"I am in a hurry. I want just a little more, I can't bear to miss anything. Just a little more—please?"

"Okay, let's see." I turned the page. It was a book that had lingered on her bedside. It had collected dust for as long as I had known her. I had never seen her pick it up. It was one of those, 'I'm going to get to it books" that no one ever did. There, collecting dust, perhaps only to impress visitors, to instill the impression of the erudite resident. Now, as a last-ditch effort to absorb its secrets, it had been recalled from ignominy for this special occasion.

"This one is by Derek Walcott, its called 'Love after Love'"

"Well there is that," the whispered voice had a hint of a smile in it. The gnome wheezed, the scaffold beeped, the clock marked the minutes.

> *"The time will come*
> *when, with elation*
> *you will greet yourself arriving*
> *at your own door, in your own mirror*
> *and each will smile at the other's welcome,*
> *and say, sit here. Eat.*
> *You will love again the stranger who*

was your self.
Give wine. Give bread. Give back
your heart
to itself, to the stranger who has
loved you
all your life, whom you ignored
for another, who knows you by
heart.
Take down the love letters from the
bookshelf,
the photographs, the desperate
notes,
peel your own image from the
mirror.
Sit. Feast on your life.

Wow, that's pretty heavy. Fitting in a way. Right?"

There was no reply. The gnome gasped and sighed out its measured breath. The small green screen hanging from the gallows silently showed a steady beating rhythm, the numbers blinked on and off. Out in the hallway, staff people laughed and planned their weekends. The clock marked the minutes. I stared down at the pages as they blurred in my vision and waited. The longer the wait, the deeper the thought that would emerge, as it always had but now in a breathy whisper

"There are those that lack the strength of character to assume such an incredible burden of integrity. Those who cannot, pass from the earth rather quickly don't they. That is why we are so unique. I see a lot of people that are tested, many have not been able to assume the mantle, their strength failed and they declined the opportunity. I feel that the power of the wise exists within each of us. No passing of the knowledge and wisdom is necessary. A shame that we realize it so late."

The voice weakened near the end of the lengthy statement. The shadowy figure in the corner, breathed its measured breath bored at its own unremarkable sameness. The gallows beeped on.

I thought about her words. So true, but irrelevant in this moment. I had waited for this moment, prayed for it and been wracked with guilt because I longed for it. I thought about the statement by someone that I'd long forgotten but remembered the spirit of it.

'I sat with my anger until it finally told me its' real name. Its real name was grief.'

I had sat with my anger. It had not developed into grief. It was still anger. I had experienced the spectrum in past times. I thought back to the other times, other struggles, the bad old days. I had walked through hell before, but to do it just so that I could be here in this chair with my damp armpits, my facial muscles feeling too tight felt cruel even by Christian standards. That spectrum of true loss, true anger, true grief and abject fear of the future. I had to say that the despair of loss was the most crushing. You may do your best to share the others, but that one...that one...is a soul crusher.

"Shall I read another?"

"Not just yet. I'm still listening to the last one in my head."

"What?"

With obvious difficulty she turned her head enough so that she could see me in her peripheral vision. The green screen marked the effort by making the little blips closer together, the monster in the corner unperturbed by anything else, exhaled another measured breath.

"You're a veteran. A Vietnam War vet. You never made it all the way home. You guys came home trained to be serial killers. People who are sympathetic enough see that journey in your eyes. It's terrifying for them. They see the struggle and feel the darkness inside of you. I'm sorry. I'm sorry that you've been alone for so long. I'm sorry that you couldn't let them in. I sorry that you wouldn't let them in. And now, you'll be alone again."

I felt my anger rise even higher. This was none of her business. I had learned that people never deserved your trust. I didn't need some naïve Utopian lecturing me. I had learned the value of solitude, in both head and heart. Easier that way. She was only the second to break through that barrier, not without a certain amount of joy and resentment on my part. The first one had taught me the bitter lesson to begin with.

Serial killer? Maybe, but still?

"Serial killer, maybe so, but that was a long time ago."

"People are afraid. They're afraid that someone will swoop in and mess with their 401k, or their insurance won't cover whatever dumbass thing they've done lately. You give-two-shits people scare them." The whispered voice was imperious, voicing urgency.

"So what? Let the sons-a-bitches do whatever they do. I've got no time for them."

"No time for them, or too lazy to become one of them?"

"Why are you trying to get my goat? I'd like to have what they have, you bet. I just can't get there the way they did. I'm not crawling over the bodies to climb to the top of that pile."

Silence.

The little green arrow ticked across the screen, the peaks increasing the distance between each other. The numbers blinked higher and then lower. The machine took a breath and wheezed it out, and then another and then another. I waited. Finally, I couldn't stand it, I had to vent.

"Okay, listen. It's like this. They look at me, or us, we 'others' and I see what they see. That recognition of lethal force that they envy, when they see it on TV, but fear it when they're standing next to it in a queue, or on a bus, killers, coping but only barely. They want a life like a sit-com, but comfortably so. Screw that."

Silence. The gnome took a breath. The cursor blipped on. Rain began to pelt the window, wiggling down the wind-blown glass. In the hall outside, pagers pinged, cart rolled by on three good wheels and one with a seizure disorder. The clocked marked the minutes, the precious seconds. Soon it would be too dark to read from the hated book.

"Would you like to hear the next one?"

"No," and then softer, "not just yet. I'm sad about what you just said.

I had reached a point where I prayed for the release of caring, to the relief where I could finally be allowed to grieve. From the very beginning I wanted to grieve but I couldn't. We knew where it would end, we knew what we would feel. But instead, I had been forced to show a brave and encouraging face while we buried our fear, dreading the future, hopeful for some foolish outcome. I had been furious this whole time, and now most especially because it was still too early to grieve.

"I'm sorry."

"I know. You've been great you know? And I love you, you should know that too. Thank you."

I squirmed in the stupid uncomfortable chair.

It had been designed with an eye to limiting the time that visitors lingered. It was suddenly even more uncomfortable.

"I love you too," I looked down at my boots ashamed that I was uncomfortable with that recognition.

A small hand emerged from under the grey sheet reaching into the space between us.

"Please? Please?"

In the shadowed room the hand, white against the starched white of sheets. Someone should have trimmed her nails. I leaned forward and took the hand its cold engulfed in the heat of mine. I held the delicate thing in the otherwise empty room. The clock blinked the minutes away, the machine in the corner wheezed in and out, bored with the monotony of its own creation.

"Are you family?"

"No."

"Close friend then?"

"Sometimes."

I knew she was looking at me, but couldn't return it. I watched the rivulets as they tracked down the window. I heard the alarms sound. I didn't have to look, I held her hand as it lost its grip. I wasn't angry anymore; I was free.

The rain on the window blurred as my tears coursed down and dripped from my chin.

No Signal

by Timothy R. Baldwin

My eyes flutter open as daylight pours into my room. It takes me a moment to get my bearings. When I do, I curse and hop out of bed. I grab a wad of clothing. Slacks and a dress shirt, both wrinkled, would have to do.

I glance at my phone.

7:58 am.

Even in my haste to throw on whatever, I will be late. Meanwhile, my students will already be in homeroom.

I grab my phone and thumb through the device. Something went wrong last night.

I freeze.

Not a single alarm exists on my phone. This, despite having the phone for some six months.

"Jeanne, did you —"

The bathroom door creaks.

I venture into the bathroom, and I am immediately bombarded with the pungent smell of sewage. I turn on the faucet. Air sputters through the valves until a splash of dark brown water pours into the tub.

Jeanne, I conclude, probably discovered the same thing this morning and ditched me to go to her place. Was I such a letdown last night that she didn't even bother to wake me?

For now, I opt to call into work. As the phone rings, I wrack my brain. There had to be a logical explanation for the phone and the apparent backup in the bathroom.

On the second ring, the school secretary answers the phone.

"It's a great day at Chesterton High School," she begins cheerfully. "How can I help you?"

"Hey, Linda. This is Alek. I was calling to —"

"Alek? What's your last name?"

"Petrov."

She shuffles through what sounds like papers. "Mr. Petrov?"

"Yes?"

"Are you late for an IEP meeting for your child?"

"No. I work there."

"What do you teach?"

"Are you kidding?" I ask.

"Science. You filed my paperwork when the school first hired me last summer."

"I'm sorry—"

"I've been working there for over a year!"

"Sir. You're going to have to calm down. I'm

sorry. I've never seen your paperwork or your name come across my desk."

"Linda, I'm not sure what's going on, but —"

"Maybe you have the wrong number?"

I exhale as I grit my teeth. "Maybe. I'll try another number."

I sit on the edge of my bed and stare at a gaping hole in the wall. Jeanne and I must've had a wild night. Only I can't remember any of it.

I do a mental walk-through of last night's events. A group of teachers from Chesterton High met up at the pub. At the end of the bar, a stunning woman eyed me with a sly smile. Josh, one of my coworkers, nudged me. My drink spilled. The woman laughed, then called the bartender over. As she ordered, she nodded toward me.

Then the bartender handed me a shot. "The lady would like to share a drink with you."

Josh nudged me off the barstool. I grabbed the drink, and my legs seemed to work of their own accord, drawing me to her.

"Sir?" A woman's voice takes me out of the moment.

The back of my throat itches. Swallowing, I lift the phone to my ear. "Yes? I'm here."

The woman chuckles. "Oh, good. I thought I lost you there, Mr. Petrov. Did you get the number?"

My eyes wander back to the hole in the wall.

"Thanks for your help."

"Have a —"

I end the call.

My thoughts go back to Jeanne as I rub my temples. I try to recall something vivid about her. Her eyes had been captivating. Yet, even these remain an abstraction to me, as though my mind's eye has gone completely blind.

I tap the phone's screen and find the email app. The inbox is empty. More to the point, no accounts are set up. Like my alarms, it's as if the entirety of my digital life has been erased. But did they account for my knowing the username and passwords of all my accounts?

I grin. I'll shoot an email to Josh. He'd be able to fill in the details of last night's escapades. I select the option to enter a new account. Like my inability to visualize the woman, the account information hovers in a blurry haze on my memory's periphery.

I sense this has happened before, not to me, per se, but to those who wish for a reboot.

Blank faces and blank papers flash in my memory as I lecture incoherently about something important. Details escape me, and I am left with the emptiness one feels years after losing a pet or loved one.

This idea of loss is the most concrete thing I've been able to recall all morning. After looking at my phone, I see the last number I dialed is still there. I open a browser and conduct a search for the number. Soon, a link to Chesterton High School's website pops up.

I call the number, and a woman's familiar and cheery voice answers on the second ring.

"Hi," I say. "This is Alek —"

"Hi, Mr. Petrov!"

My heart flutters. *Is that recognition in Linda's voice?*

"Did you figure things out?" she adds before I can respond.

Recognition. Yes. But not because the woman knows me.

I hang up.

Another idea comes to my mind. I've kept paper records of every bank statement I've ever gathered. Even my birth certificate and passport are all locked safely away in a —

My eyes drift to the hole in the wall. I swallow a burning lump in my throat, and it travels with acidic foreboding to the pit of my stomach. Whatever happened, happened last night. Someone, probably the woman I brought home, drugged me. Then, they found my place of employment and my accounts and systematically eradicated my existence in some sick social experiment.

I needed to move. Whoever did this couldn't be too far ahead of me.

I launch my phone and watch with satisfaction

as it shatters to pieces. Then I sift through the remains and find the SIM card. This, too, I destroy, making it that much more difficult for anyone to track me.

I enter the hallway and make my way downstairs. My nostrils flair as I breathe in thick, moldy air.

The living room walls are bare. Clear plastic layered with dust covers furniture that isn't mine. I flip the switch, but the lights don't work. I go to the kitchen, and my stomach growls at the sight of the refrigerator. When I open it, rot and mold incite my gag reflexes. I slam the door shut.

None of this makes sense. This is my house. Almost every part of it is familiar, but the paint is faded and peeling. It seems no one, including myself, has lived in this house for years.

But wasn't it just last night that I came home from a bar? With a woman, even? I'd like to say we had a good time, but I can't remember. It's as if I exist in a time warp where past and present overlap. Still, a subtle memory tugs at the corner of my mind, just out of reach with hues of blues and reds.

Dance music begins with a steady drumbeat. Patrons, Josh, and my coworkers begin gyrating on the dance floor. The woman, Jeanne, leans into me. She smells of sweat and vanilla.

"Hey," she says. "Wanna dance?"

I down my drink. "Let's go."

I take her hand, and lights flash around me. Shading my eyes, I turn to her.

She's gone.

A glare catches on the front blinds of the house. I rush to the window and disrupt a layer of dust as I yank on the drawstring. The blinds crash to the floor, and I jump away. Through the haze of the window, I spot my car. Rust speckles its faded blue paint. The driveway pavement is caked with crabgrass, and seedlings have taken root in several large cracks. The rest of the neighborhood is old—maybe by thirty years. Vacant houses with caved-in roofs seem to frown at me. My house is the only one with a car in the driveway.

The air inside the living room swelters and drives me outside, where the air carries with it the scent of fire. As I glance from one end of the street to the other, I am flooded with images of a past I never experienced. An ancient explosion rocks the house, and glass shatters from within. Strange that this would be the first vivid memory to divide a blank canvas incapable of nothing more than the idea of a thing.

A scream breaks the silence of the neighborhood. I turn in time to see a figure of a woman running away from me. She glances back, and I catch her profile.

Jeanne!

Her dark hair swishes as she returns her

attention to avoiding obstacles that line the streets. She leaps over a downed electrical pole and plods on.

"Wait!" I call out.

She keeps running until she vanishes like a desert mirage.

"Jeanne!"

Abandoned houses mock me as they echo back my cry of desperation. I don't bother to call out again but run, leaping over the downed electrical pole toward Jeanne's vanishing point. Plodding on, I ignore the sting of brush and branches whipping against my arms and face. Beneath me, my feet continue to pound against concrete.

When the path thins out, a massive, spoked wheel silhouetted by the sun's glare looms before me. I squint and take care to traverse the loose concrete beneath me. A large pavilion to my left houses rusted-out bumper cars beneath a dilapidated roof. To my right, a four-wheeled cart with faded red and off-white stripes leans on one broken wheel. Weeds and shattered glass seem to overtake the cart.

"Do you like what you see?" A female voice whispers with the breeze, and I spin at the sound of metallic creaking.

My sudden movement sends the pounding of a late-night hangover to my forehead. I blink back tears in my struggle to see even the phantom of life.

"Jeanne!" I call out. "Where are you?"

Her figure, beautiful and radiant, flashes. She is sitting in a bumper car, beckoning me with a pat on the seat beside her. Then she's gone. Music to my right fires off a rapid tempo, up and down, and the ground beneath me rumbles to the sound of a ride gearing up.

A red warning light flashes as a gate lowers. Sitting in a driver's seat, I stew in the idea of waiting.

Beside me, Jeanne gives me a faraway look and speaks with sensual pleasure. "Do you want to go for a ride?" She reaches her hand out to my face. "No, you wouldn't last."

A train passes, each car is graffitied with the characters of a language I recognize but don't understand. Gradually and simultaneously, the train rusts until it screeches to a halt. Something brushes against my face, tickling my cheek. A breeze passes over me, and the thing flutters away. Somewhere beyond my reach, it has gotten itself caught and now flaps in the wind.

The pain in my frontal lobe travels to the back of my head, flooding my body until I realize I am lying face up on the ground. I open my eyes and see the sun has traveled beyond high noon. With a groan, I sit up.

"Do *you* want to go for a ride?" Her question is more persistent this time.

I look up at the Ferris wheel. Ghostly

memories play tricks on me. Couples in love laugh and swing on the top of the wheel, then they are consumed in a white-hot blaze. Memory overlays memory of a time past that I am damned sure I've never experienced.

But, unlike the carnival, filled with forgotten experiences, I seem to have ceased to exist in the world. Or, perhaps the world as I knew it has ceased to exist. I look at my hands. They are still young and smooth. The idea of passing out papers comes to me, as does the idea of caressing a woman's naked soft curves.

In my sudden sense of loss, I rise and turn my attention to a piece of paper flapping beneath a shard of glass. It tugs with lifelike familiarity, flashing words and images.

The ground crackles beneath my feet. Around me, the air begins to buzz, rising and falling in crescendo as a siren blares. I step on the corner of the pamphlet and kick away the shard of glass.

Flipping over the pamphlet as I pick it up, I cannot help but smile. It is an invitation to the amusement park. A Ferris wheel, tall and proud amongst much smaller attractions, insights images of a wife and children. She holds a stick of cotton candy as the children pull off one greedy bite after another. All at once, my mouth salivates as the air carries with it the salty sweetness of carnival treats.

Just as suddenly, ash, smokey and charred,

fills my mouth and lungs. An explosion rocks the earth, sending me back to the ground. Around me, silhouettes of mothers clutching babies run through the smoke and ash, their cries drowned out by the cacophony around us.

Tears flood my eyes and stream down my cheeks. My heart races, and I collapse to the ground. Around me, the beeping grows louder, steadily increasing as if in time with my heartbeat. I struggle to breathe as my body convulses.

"We're losing him," a woman shouts. "Someone get the defibrillator."

"It may be too late for that," a man's voice, cold and emotionless, says.

My eyes flutter in my struggle to awaken from this nightmare. I gasp.

"Alek," the woman's voice echoes.

"Jeanne?" I groan.

Her voice is far away. "Hook me up. I'm going in."

"You can't!" The man shouts. Urgency has replaced his lack of emotion. "Jeanne! Get back here. The system is already overloaded."

"This was my experiment," she says. "Mine! You hear me?"

"I said —"

White space interrupts him. I'm weightless in an all too familiar blank canvas. Soon, it's rebuilding itself in pixelated pieces. Blurred bodies twirl around me, and my hand grips a shot glass filled with brown liquid vibrating in time to the music around me.

"Alek?" a woman's voice says.

I take in Jeanne's dark, striking eyes. They narrow with concern.

"What?" I say with hesitation. "Where was I?"

Jeanne looks away. "Shit!"

I toss the shot glass to the side, not caring at all when a bar patron curses at me. I grab Jeanne's shoulders and force her to look at me.

"What the fuck happened?"

Her face pixelates and blurs with static. "I'm sorry," her voice glitches. She turns, calling to an invisible companion. "We're losing him again."

She and the bar flicker out, suddenly replaced by the graffiti I'd seen on the train cars. I grasp at the outer limits of my education and recognize the series of ones and zeros. I study their patterns as they flash around me, moving more rapidly than any human eye can read. I lock onto a shutdown. I force my will upon it, rewriting it faster than it can execute.

Soon, I regain my sight and find myself staring at Jeanne as she taps rapidly at a keyboard. She wears a white lab coat, and her thick black hair is tied up in a bun.

"Jeanne?" I ask, but my voice sounds wrong and metallic.

She looks up. A nervous smile plays at the corner of her lips. "Alek, you're back."

"Back?" I ask. I raise an arm and catch a glimpse of a steel skeletal structure. "Where's my body?"

"We have synthetic skin to cover that," Jeanne says quickly. "And we can make adjustments to your voice."

I grit what I take to be my teeth. "I don't want this."

"With some rehabilitation," she says. "You'll be fine."

"No!" I shout. Rising, I approach her. "Where's my real body?"

Jeanne backs away, blabbing something about a blast no organic body could withstand.

"He's going to self-destruct," a man shouts.

That, I realize, is the sanest thing I've experienced in recent memory. The command is easy to find within my database, and I begin the countdown.

Ten...

Nine...

"Please, Alek," Jeanne says.

Seven...

"Get out of there," a man shouts.

Five...

She yanks a drive out of the computer and takes off through a steel door.

Two...

The door bolts with a resounding thud behind her. Then, the explosion.

A red light blinks three times, and I whir to life. A message flashes across my console: *Alright, Alek, we're trying this again. This time, I promise we won't lose the signal.*

The red light blinks once, and I type back: *No signal. The experiment has failed.*

The Battle of the Change

• • ● • ·

by J.W. Bell

"Chi. Wake now, Chi!" I barely heard the voice, but the rough shake woke me to horror. Thankfully, I hadn't collapsed into a full-fledged sleep and plopped onto the table. From that, my friend Wu saved me. I shook the vivid memory of a dream from my mind while I tried to wipe the puddle of my drool from the table.

The twang in the Master's voice irritated even the air. "Li Chan? Did you hear me?"

As though the sound came from afar, my ears pulled me in the direction of the old man. He stood just under the roof and still inside of where the wall would be if we ever finished the building. His face turned towards me, and by the lamp, near him, I could better see his beak of a nose. The outline had the shape of a hawk swooping to disembowel.

I sat up straight and as smoothly as possible rubbed my chin to get rid of the gob of spit hanging there. The old man will skin me if he suspects my nap.

The breeze carried not only the smell of cooking rice and fish stew but the night soil used for fertilizer in the garden. The odors fought for dominance. The garlic lacing the stew made my mouth water, but the foulness of the human waste in the plant food spoiled that. I tried to focus on the food, not the stench. As a compromise, I concentrated on the rice paddy water with its green but promising bouquet.

Next to me, I heard the constant tap of Wu's feet on the dirt floor. The Master shuffled towards us, and both the speed and fashion of his feet kicking up the dirt sounded like his bladder would burst any second. I tried not to snicker, but all older men have trouble holding their water.

The yellow morning sky made a silhouette of him as it illuminated the valley between the terraced mountainsides. I could not see the Master's arms. He had to have tucked them behind his back. I wanted to think his hands held the discipline stick behind him. Otherwise, they would be in front and under his robes, a quicker way to issue a punishing thwack.

Maybe the discipline stick isn't with him. I liked that thought. Perhaps he had hold of his rod? He was an older man. I didn't know if I chuckled or trembled at the thought. Yuck.

I could feel the man's sharp eyes slicing into

me. "I will ask again. Who, or what is at fault if an order has not been obeyed?" The pause in his speech cut more than the sharpness of the sound. "Li Chan?"

The man stood before the pair of us. His hands were indeed behind his back. Good.

I took a deep breath, meant to appear as a cleansing breath as they taught us, but it was a stall. I'm sure it looked good. Then I answered. "Uh, the fault of the soldier." I tried to appear confident. My eyes flicked to Wu and back, but the action did no good. Wu looked to the floor, possibly for a way to escape.

The only warning I had was the whistle the rod made before the sting of the stick on my shoulder. My arm trembled, but I didn't dare raise it.

"Sun Tzu wrote: 'The first thing the commander must consider is his order.'" That twang in his voice buffeted me. "Did he communicate the order correctly? He must re-issue the order. After that, he will be sure It was not his fault. Once that is done." His voice trailed away, and I peered up at him.

His hook of a bird beak appeared to sniff the air as his black-on-black eyes focused beyond the school grounds. With what seemed to be a self-conscious breath, he straightened to his full height, a half-finger breadth taller than usual. His undivided attention now skewered on a growing commotion near the line of trees surrounding our compound.

I turned too. We all did.

It had been half a week since our conscription, and we were only about twelve years of age. The only thing I knew was that I was now in a place of *Yinyáng,* where fortune changes to the opposite of what it was at the whim of payment and repayment for things done or not done.

A large man backed into the clearing. He fought hard, but several soldiers forced him back. He was a huge spectacle, dealing death with each blow of his sword. I could hear his sword thunking into shields as he backed. He wore an armor of boiled leather, the kind I had only heard about, and to my unpracticed eye, it looked as if the cost had been high. It had taken many Kai Yuan to balance the scale of that merchant.

His enemies pressed him hard, forcing their way into the clearing. Arrows flew, some aflame, arcing high towards the huts.

"Disburse," yelled the Master as he picked up his bow and quiver. With deadly arrows flying in our direction, he stood still as a tree, fired twice before moving, and then ran not away but towards the fight.

Wu and I dropped to the ground, crawled through the open-air school, and searched for a way to run the other way. The forest beckoned. The two of us were expected to fight, of course, but we were new to soldiering. Two days, maybe three.

The battle grew faster than I could run to the trees. Masses of enemy poured into the clearing, this time from our side. My head spun to pick another direction, but the motherless pig fuckers had surrounded us.

I grabbed Wu and crawled behind the burning oak tree next to the Master's hut. The flaming leaves dropped on the roof, spreading their flames. Thick smoke surrounded the camp, dense enough for Wu and me to hide in, but it also made both of us cough.

I stood at the edge of the smoke, able to see the fight had turned into a slaughter. Other boys from our class were slaughtered, cut down equally with swords and flaming arrows.

The Master was fearless, never hesitating to kill in any way he could. Blood sprayed everywhere around him. For the first time, I smelled the mix of burning forest and flesh, with the sharp tang of blood and human viscera over the top of it all.

Three of our friends managed to evade death, two were wounded in their arms, and the last had a bleeding thigh. I waved them behind our smokescreen, and then I stepped out to encourage more to join us.

Amid all the screams and guttural moans, a wind gust forced a massive draft of the stench to roll over us, this time the smell had shit mixed within. The carnage almost overwhelmed us all. I watched a few boys puke. I could hear several retching behind me.

I turned to the boys. "Grab rocks and sticks. We have to attack."

"I'm too scared." It was one of the bigger boys, the one I thought to be the meanest. I saw where he'd wet himself.

"I don't care!" Although it wasn't quite a yell, he could tell I meant it. I'd grabbed a stick with a jagged edge to it and held it like a knife.

"They will kill us," whined another.

"They will anyway." Then an idea seemed to whisper in my head. "The enemy can't kill us if we attack at the same time."

"But–"

I stabbed the big boy in his stomach just below his ribs. It didn't pierce him, but he had trouble breathing. My eyes dared them all to challenge me." After another moment, while they stood in the foul sounds and smells, all of them bowed in understanding.

By now, smoke billowed from the tree above us right down the trunk, through the wood, and it had an odd brightness to it. The fire would engulf it soon.

I crawled to the edge of the hut and studied the battle. The Master fought near the big man who defended himself as the point of an arrow into the action. But the two warriors were about to be overcome. They hacked and stabbed as best they could, but I could see they were tiring.

I turned back to the boys. "Do not yell until we are almost on them. I'll signal. If you can, grab a sword or arrow to use as a weapon. A spear would be great. A sword should aim for the neck, arrow the inner thigh, and spear the chest or gut." I waved them closer to me. "Ready!"

I scrambled through the smoke curtain, and the others trailed. "Go." Although I yelled it, the sound wouldn't carry over the battle noises, so I ran back and stabbed one in the butt with my stick. The tactic worked.

I used that same branch to slap all the boys in the shoulder or back as I returned to the front of them all. We attacked in a straight line like an arrow in flight.

No one noticed the band of boys sprinting across the compound. I seized, first a spear, and then snatched a half arrow. I bit down on the shaft and held it between my teeth. The spear I held ready to stab. Wu grabbed a sword. One boy tried to pick up an ax, but it was heavy, and he left it.

"Run!" I yelled. He snatched a knife instead.

The crash and bluster of the fighting men were so loud it hurt my ears.

"Attack!" I screamed as loud as I could and keep the arrow in my teeth. We joined the battle as one, stabbing, slashing, and gouging the enemy. But no blood showed. We were like gnats on a rabid dog.

One man swiped his arm through the air and sent us all sprawling. I'd lost my spear, and my nose bled. "Get him!" I screamed.

I leaped to his back and stabbed at his neck, pushing the point down into his chest, but I could not pull the arrow free.

He dropped and blood spurted over me. I ignored the goop, pulled the man's sword free, and slashed as hard as I could, not caring who I hit. The solid thunk of the blade hacking flesh and bone jarred my arm, and I pulled it free.

I don't know what the other boys did, but in my mind, I knew what to do.

I'd found myself behind the man that fought the Master and hacked a solid blow just below his knee. Blood erupted, and he dropped. Another took his place. The Master slashed downward, striking his attacker between the neck and shoulder just as I stabbed the man's ribs. The point of the Master's blade dragged down my forehead, slicing a deep cut. It burned like a fire brand, but I continued the attack.

The Master's opponent fell, trapping my sword as he did, yanking it from my hand.

I grabbed a knife from the ground and renewed my attacked, stabbing and gouging. I punched the men around me until I reached the armored man the Master had gone to protect. Up close, the man was huge, grunting, and stopping life with every stroke.

He shoved me to the ground and slashed the air above me with another grunt, and then his foot pushed me down again, and he kept it there — his immense weight bearing down, trapping me.

My ears told me the fight raged above, and I could neither fight nor escape. The stench of burning wood, bloody ground, and charred bodies filled my nostrils. And blood covered me head to toe while I lay in the muck.

The foot released me when two or three bodies lurched at the big man, knocking him to the ground. The Master, too, was down. The enemy swarmed.

I screamed for the boys to see if any yet lived. The sound of clubs beating the two men filled the battle noise.

I grabbed a club and whacked an attacker. From my left came another thunk. More pummeling happened around me. I took a club to my legs, crumpling me to the ground, but I still fought, not done. On the way down I hit yet another enemy, this time in his balls.

Then the last thump.

~

I woke to the smell of tainted broth under my nose. My stomach rebelled, but firm hands grabbed my chin and nose. Too weak to fight, and as I gulped for breath, someone poured putrid liquid into my mouth. Vomit burned my throat but never reached my mouth because I swallowed again and coughed, ragged and deep.

My head ached as if an ax had split it.

The soft chuckling of an old woman filled my ears, and I turned towards the sound. There she stood, wrinkled skin, hair as brittle as straw, and her smile so wide I could see the gap from where she missed two teeth on the top of her mouth.

As she noticed my eyes were open, her face fell, her eyes opened, and she bowed a deep, lingering bow, as if she'd done it facing a far superior person of rank.

The bow chilled me. I was a peasant.

Then I became aware of someone else in the hut. I didn't want to appear curious, so I lay waiting for the dignitary to present himself.

Nothing happened. Nor could I hear anything.

After long minutes through which my thoughts raged, trying to figure out what was happening, I started to rise from the pallet. But as soon as I moved, the ancient woman screeched and became agitated. Another cough racked me. She shuffled to a table and poured a cup of barley tea, held it forward, and offered it.

I raised my head to drink, taking a moment to scan the room by eye. Not only was there no one else in the room, but I also didn't recognize the place. I'd never seen a thing like it.

She forced me to drink, not the way the vile brew had gone down but held the cup to my lips until I sipped. The barley tea made me feel like I might live.

I looked at the cup and stared. Something was different. Then I knew. I could only see from one eye.

"Are you at peace, Li Chan?" A Basso's voice spoke the traditional Korean greeting.

Without thinking, I nodded. "Yes." Then I turned to the right to see who spoke, my blind side. I tried to turn, but a hand pressed on my shoulder to push me down to the mat. It was the big soldier. He now squatted next to me, and I could see him if I turned my head.

The Master squatted next to him and spoke, "We know your father is Korean, and your mother, is Chinese, Chan." The twang in his voice made my head hurt.

The big man grunted and stared at the Master. "Master Chong, and I want to know whose family name you took."

My legs and arms trembled. I felt like a dead rat. "Venerable sir, I have taken my mother's name." Then I added, "Custom allows for it, sir."

A deep rumbling chuckle and a large hand patted me. "That is true, Li Chan. That is true." He leaned down towards me, stopped, and then walked to my other side, the side on which I could see well. "You fought splendidly yesterday."

I stared at him. "Sir, I have no idea–"

He held his hand in front of his mouth, palm towards me. "Li Chan, where did you learn what you did?"

That confused me even more. The Master had been schooling all of us. "I don't know what you mean?" I started to rise.

Master's lanky arm shot out and pushed me back down. He didn't care if I was sick or not. "You will address General Ho respectfully. Sir, or General, or–"

A big hand grabbed the Master's arm. "Li Chan. Not only did you follow Sun Tzu's advice to strive for surprise and disorient our enemy, but you also commanded your soldiers to attack as one in the line. It resulted in the massing of harm brought to the enemy. It was decisive and led to their defeat."

The general leaned back onto his heels, and his brows furrowed. The expression made his round face wrinkle, but his eyes sparkled. "I want to know how you arrived at what to do?"

I reached for my head to scratch it, and the old crone started screeching. She leaned over me shaking her finger and screamed in a dialect which I did not understand.

The general laughed and waved the air in front of him. "She says you need to leave your bandages alone. Your wound needs to heal before you take them away."

"Is this why my eye won't work?"

The Master waved the air. "Your eye is fine. The bandage for your face wound covers it, though. It is the *Dao*."

I relaxed further onto the floor. "My eye is good?"

The basso rumble again. "Of course, Li Chan. You will have a fearsome scar, and your eye will still see. Now, how did you arrive at the idea to attack the way you did?"

I swallowed. "An idea. I had an idea, like my voice telling me what to do."

Both men sat back, entirely on their haunches. The general's eyes shot around the strange room, finally coming to rest on the Master. The skinny man had chewed the inside of his cheek during that time. As their eyes connected, each gave the other an almost imperceptible nod, and the general spoke, "This is a scarce moment, one where you know your *yinyáng*," he nodded to me, "eumyang if you prefer the Korean word for it. Your eumyang has changed. You will stay with me."

He worked his way to his feet and chuckled as he did. "Old bones." His laughter resounded through the room. "Master Chong!"

The Master turned his beak towards the general.

"You will outfit the boys conscripted with him. Their training will be how to guard him."

"Sir?"

"Yes, Li."

"What is this place, this room?" The direction of my eye showed him the small, glorious room I lay in."

He grunted. "It is my quarters. My soldiers carry it. It goes wherever we march. You will have one yourself." His teeth gleamed with cleverness. "In time."

He strode from the room.

The Master jumped up, gave a deep nod towards me, and held it for a heartbeat. The bow to an honored equal. Then he followed the general out. The ancient woman cackled while walking around, chattering like a chipmunk.

Keep Away

by Jake Cavanah

Matt clicked the safety on and strapped the rifle over his shoulder. He jumped out of the tree and landed on a bumpy root hidden under a layer of crunchy leaves, sending a sharp pain through his knee. He tried running, then compromised on an accelerated walk.

Matt used his arms to shield his face from the blackberry bushes and the low tree branches pointy enough to poke an eye out. It wasn't until making it through a dense part of the forest he realized he was almost at the bank of the river that ran through the back of the property, which, unbeknownst to him, meant he was close to a mile away from the house. Noble firs blocked his view, but, after a week of rain, he could hear the river's current through the trees. Water crashing against the rocks echoed through the valley, so deafening that Matt could hardly hear himself panting.

To both his left and right, there was about one hundred yards of flat land between him and more brush similar to what he just came through, but, still, no Wilson.

Matt rested his hands atop his head so his lungs had room to expand, but the cold burning sensation attacking his chest wouldn't go away.

All he wore was a camouflage crew neck his grandpa had given him, sweats from school, and waterproof hunting boots he found in the garage. All unsuitable for the conditions.

"Matt, over here! Hurry, over here!"

His cousin was a notch higher than the river.

Matt started towards him and nearly face-planted after slipping on some wet, jagged rocks hiding under the weeds. He stuck his arms out just before his entire body hit the ground, but not before both shins met a rock's sharp edge. It cut open his sweats and left a couple gashes that sent blood trickling down his legs.

Uncomfortable, freezing, and in pain, Matt's irritation with Wilson was only increasing.

"Put that down," Matt said when he finally made it over to his younger cousin.

Wilson didn't register what Matt was referring to until he said it more sternly a second time.

"Where is she?" Matt asked. He picked up the rifle and pointed it downwards.

Wilson led him along an unkempt trail that took them to the river, where Sally was inches from the water fighting to stay awake.

Or, better yet, alive.

"What should we do?" Wilson asked.

Matt crouched down and scratched the top of Sally's head. The bullet had gone through her shoulder, so he took his crew neck off and gently covered her wound with it.

She whimpered at first, but then, relaxed and let him care for her.

"I—I—it was—it was an accident. I thought she was something else," Wilson said.

"I'll go get Grandpa," Matt said.

"What?"

Matt repeated himself over the thunderous river.

"What are we going to tell him?"

"That the river took her."

Matt tossed Sally in and said, "And that you went after her."

"Wai—"

Matt threw his cousin in and watched the water carry them towards the waterfall.

Starting Over

by Kasey Rogers

The sound of a car horn startled Julie. She was so deep in thought she didn't notice that traffic had slowed down, and most of it was merging from three lanes into one to take the ramp off I-87 to the Albany International Airport. Julie chastised herself for being so distracted and gave the driver in the next lane an apologetic look. Signaling, she tried to move ahead of him to exit as well. He flipped her the bird and maneuvered his truck forward, blocking her ability to join the cars already in line.

"Thanks, pal!" she muttered under her breath.

Usually, she would have returned the rude gesture. But she was not in the mood to deal with morons today. It was a day she had been anticipating for weeks and one that she knew would soon change her life. Nothing today would deter her from her mission.

It began months ago when she realized that her routine of drinking too much wine and watching whatever British police procedural she could find on Netflix was getting old. Night after night, she curled up on the couch alone. She longed for companionship. Glancing at the mantle above her fireplace, she saw a picture of Doug beaming back at her. His blazing smile and deep brown eyes still melted her heart. Julie missed him more now than ever. For years, she was reluctant to start over. She knew she would never find another Doug. When her former college roommate hinted that perhaps it was time to let go, it got Julie thinking.

"Your garden looks great!" Allison commented on a post Julie made on Facebook one day.

Julie liked her comment and replied, "That's because I zoomed in on the flowers and not all the weeds I still have to pull. I had to stop. Every muscle in my body aches."

"Let's face it, we're getting old," Allison wrote back.

"It's hard to remember the days Doug and I would hike for hours, and then I'd come home refreshed instead of feeling like a bag of rocks!" Julie replied.

"He's been gone a long time. I know starting over is tough, but maybe it's something to consider?" Allison added with a dozen heart emojis and smiley faces.

Julie never replied. She couldn't explain how difficult that was. Even thinking about starting over caused a great deal of apprehension. Taking the steps necessary to fill the void left when he died of a cancer that ravaged his body seemed impossible. The pain of losing him lingered for years. Whenever she turned in for the night, she missed the warmth that once came from the other side of the bed. As often as she had teased him for snoring or waking her when he got up to get a drink or such, she yearned to have him there beside her. Sometimes, she rolled over to snuggle closer to him before realizing he was gone. The two of them did so much together. It seemed impossible to forget all the things she adored about him. As Julie moved through life alone, she felt his absence daily.

Maybe it is time to start something new? Her friend was right. It was time to let go.

Still, questions overshadowed her desires. She had been looking forward to her pending retirement. But the prospects of facing it alone now made her pause. Julie tried to convince herself she'd adjust. After all—she could finally start traveling.

But what fun was that if I have to do it by myself? Thoughts of a solitary life made the future more daunting.

If she moved forward, she knew she would be making a huge commitment. And what about compatibility? Doug's passing left her set in her ways. She was used to a low-key, rather sedentary life now. Every time she even thought about how much things would change, she became hesitant. Embarking on such an endeavor was an enormous decision. She talked herself out of moving ahead multiple times. Lately, though, the aching feeling for something more prompted her to put her hesitancy aside. After all, as Allison reminder her, she wasn't getting any younger. She decided it wouldn't hurt to take a peek at a few websites; no harm done if things never progressed further than that. Julie got out her laptop and began her search online for her ideal companion.

It was hard to know where to start. There were so many sites out there—all with such alluring profiles filled with fabulous pictures and exciting descriptions of possible matches. Julie focused on sites that best suited her criteria. Once she narrowed it down to one or two websites with the widest selection of profiles that interested her, she entered her personal information. She filled her evenings by immersing herself in personality traits, likes, dislikes and considerations of where they lived and their individual histories. She eliminated most of them because so few matched her list of expectations.

Many of the profiles corresponded with some of what she was looking for—but only one of them tick all the boxes. Night after night, she came back to one profile repeatedly. His name was Gus. His description indicated he was mature, hardworking, good-natured, and recently retired. He loved the outdoors and wasn't fond of cats. There was something about his picture that melted Julie's heart. Perhaps it was his graying beard and soulful brown eyes. She couldn't help but notice—he reminded her a little of Doug. After careful consideration, she had reason to believe, just perhaps she'd found a perfect match.

The next day at work, Julie tried hard to contain her excitement. By the time lunch came around, she was dying to tell someone. When Wendy, one of her co-workers, came into the lunchroom and sat down next to her, Julie casually brought Gus into their conversation.

"How was your weekend?" Wendy asked, sitting down with a thermos of soup she took out of her lunch bag. Julie smiled. "It was good. How about yours?"

"Same ole, same ole," Wendy responded. "Although Joe had the kids this weekend, so I had a bit of time to myself for a change." Wendy glanced across the table, then studied Julie's face. "Judging from the grin on your face, yours was more than good. Fess up, Julie. I've known you long enough to tell something is up."

Julie showed Wendy a picture of Gus and told her all about him.

"He's quite handsome, don't you think?" Julie asked her. Her heart sank when Wendy responded less enthusiastically than she expected.

"Is it smart at your age to start something new?" Wendy asked her.

"Why not? I'm not that old! Besides, it's something I've thought about for quite a while," Julie said, a bit more defensively than she meant to.

"It's just that you've been alone for a long time. And didn't you tell me a few months ago that once you retire, you plan to see the world? What if he's not the type that likes to travel? Man, if I were in your shoes, I'd never make that type of commitment," Wendy added.

"Well, you're not in my shoes. Plus, I haven't decided yet. It's just something I'm considering," Julie told her.

"Hey, I'm not trying to be a wet blanket, but be careful. I know lots of people who've regretted doing the same thing. They get caught up in the warm fuzzy feeling of it all but forget the realities," Wendy warned.

"It's just that Gus seems perfect for me," Julie told her. "But, perhaps you're right," she conceded. "I'll think about it."

For more than a week, Julie let Wendy get into her head. Everything about Gus soon became an obstacle in her mind. She armed herself with dozens of reasons it was a bad idea to pursue things further.

He is older than I was initially thinking about, she told herself. *He's all the way down in Atlanta, for God's sake! The distance alone makes all of this way too complicated. What if he's not so perfect after all?*

She stopped going online. The next weekend, instead, she found a new British procedural and binge-watched the first ten episodes. But murder and mayhem, even with a British accent, couldn't erase the images of Gus in Julie's mind. She tried harder and harder to convince herself it wasn't a good idea after all. However, she couldn't stop thinking about him.

Then one night after work, she logged into her email, and there he was. Gus was featured on the list with several other profiles from the site she'd registered with weeks ago. His picture was just as alluring as it was the first time she saw it. He seemed to call to her. She couldn't help but think she'd given in to her fear instead of following her heart's desire.

She put her worries aside, and all the hurdles she imagined disappeared. Julie made arrangements to pick him up a few weeks later at the baggage claim area at the Albany International Airport. On the passenger's seat, she had his picture—the one she'd downloaded from the website along with all the information about his flight and what time to pick him up. Julie was nervous and excited, but more than anything, she was happy she didn't wait too long. Whatever happened, she would live with her decision.

Julie arrived at the planned destination and stood anxiously wait as others grab their bags off the carousel. She peered down the hallway and saw a small cluster of people approaching. They were smiling. She knew instinctively, it must be him. Then she saw him through the crowd.

He looks exactly like he did in his picture.

At that moment, Julie knew she made the right decision. Any doubts she had disappeared. He looked straight at her and approached with reserved confidence.

Maybe he was longing for me as much as I was for him?

Meeting his gaze, Julie walked toward him, ignoring the flight attendant walking by his side.

"Are you Julie Worthington?" the flight attendant asked when she reached them.

"That's me!" Julie told her.

"You're a lucky woman."

"I know," Julie told her. Julie took time to relish the moment. She looked deeply into Gus's eyes. She was flooded with emotion when he looked back at her and express a sense of complete joy. Gently taking his leash, Julie gave him a quick pat on the head and rubbed the big Sheppard behind his ears.

"He's a real keeper," the attendant told her.

"I knew he would be. He's a retired police dog!" Julie said, beaming with pride. "Come on, Gus! We're going home."

The One Handed Rower of Myonnesus

• • ⬤ • •

by D. Krauss

Alcidas didn't murder Phrynus, merely lopped off his hand, but that wasn't mercy; it was weariness. Cutting the throats of 200 mariners was exhausting business. "Just cripple them," Alcidas gestured at the twenty or so still left, Phrynus among them, and stumbled drunkenly away. Lying on the dock afterwards holding his stump, Phrynus knew the greater mercy was a cut throat. When he caught up with Alcidas, he would provide that.

Alcidas and his Spartan pirates took off the next morning, where, no one knew, and Phrynus was thrown in the hold of a merchanter that made its cautious way out of Myonnesus. The pilot feared what had befallen Phrynus' ship and, consequently, made a roundabout, slow return to Athens. By the time they docked, Phrynus was the only one of his maimed compatriots still alive.

And barely that. He was comatose from the raging infection in his left hand and could not tell the compassionate, but practical, pilot who he was or where to take him so they left him at the spring of Asclepios. The acolytes bathed Phrynus' stump daily until the putrescence subsided and hard scarring formed. At some point, he came awake and, at a later point, left, thanking the acolytes and promising a substantial sacrifice of gold and crowing cocks when his fortunes returned. The acolytes shrugged and went back to work; a one-handed rower had no prospects of fortune.

Phrynus weaved through the Parthenon and the crowds of refugees escaping the Spartan scourge, careful to avoid the filth of their camps and the contentious groups demanding release to attend farms that were, no doubt, already burned. It took him until nightfall to reach his own house and he walked straight in, startling Hestia, who thought him a shade come to complain about his lack of burial. After finally grasping the situation, she wished he had been a shade. "How will we eat?" she wailed, pointing at his handless left arm. The children joined her, knowing they would soon have to cull the trash heaps outside the refugee camps and along the Long Walls to find food and would become the laughing stock of their former friends. Phrynus looked at her, considered how ill named she was, and left.

He made his way to the other side of the Parthenon where one of Lysias' smelters was located. Cyril, a particularly adept greave maker, worked there and, fortuitously, was at the forge pouring bronze when Phrynus approached. "Rower," Cyril greeted.

Phrynus held up his stump. "I want you to make me a hand."

Cyril's eyebrows rose. "Misfortunes of war?"

Phrynus nodded. "I want to replace it."

"Best you pray that Zeus grow you another. Or find a trireme intent on making circles." Cyril chuckled at his own witticism.

"I want you to make me another hand."

Cyril eyed him. "I could. It would be a thing of beauty. But there is no way to attach it." He pointed at Phrynus' stump.

"Attach it the way you would a greave."

Cyril considered that and nodded. "Seven drachmas."

Phrynus swayed at the expense. "Three drachmas, three obols," he countered.

"You understand the craftsmanship involved?" Cyril feigned insult. "Five drachmas, one obol."

They settled on four drachmas and two obols, a little more than half a week's wage for Cyril, quite satisfying to him, and the last of Phrynus' savings, which was not satisfying to Hestia. "What are you doing?" she cried when, at the end of the agreed upon week, he withdrew the coins from the floor trap and prepared to meet Cyril. "We will starve!"

"We will not," he said to assure her, leaving out that starvation depended on the fit of the new hand and the willingness of a pilot to take on a maimed rower. Good chances for both, considering Cyril's reputation and the casualties suffered this far.

Cyril met him at the entrance. "I am a humble man," he said while Phrynus kept a straight face, "but this is a masterpiece." He flourished a box of acacia, a nice touch, and opened it. A hand of bronze lay snug in wool, cords wrapped around it in a pleasing manner, the fingers of the hand gathered at the thumb in a closed circle. "Let me show you," Cyril took it out and turned it onto Phrynus' stump, cold against the flap. Expertly, he wrapped the cords about Phrynus' chest, gathering the ends about the opposing elbow. "You can loosen or tighten the cords as required," and Cyril showed him how− lift an elbow to tighten, flip the stump to ease. "Practice it," Cyril ordered and Phrynus did, alternately pulling and loosing the cords until he could keep the hand snug against his stump even during the wildest of maneuvers. "It will hold either oar or spear," Cyril said and showed him the most clever of innovations- the closed circle of the hand popped out, the bronze circlet dangling from a hidden chain, adjusting the hand to different shafts.

"Wrap the chain when you hold a spear," Cyril warned, "or your stabbing will drive it out."

Phrynus could barely breathe. "It is a thing of beauty."

"As I said."

"You have made me a whole man."

"In only your eyes."

Phrynus gave the coins to Cyril. "It is all I have."

"As agreed."

"I would give you more…"

Cyril smiled. "Tell the other maimed. That's worth a drachma in itself."

Phrynus headed towards Piraeus. He got there in the late evening and slept on a dock until morning. He asked a netter about Admiral Paches and got directions. The admiral's pilot was standing next to the piers, supervising the ship fittings. Shouts of men combined with the washing of triremes just pulled from the depths. Phrynus nodded approval. Clean vessels were fast vessels.

"Do you seek Alcidas?" Phrynus asked.

"We do," the pilot, Teutiaplas, said. "He goes to Patmos."

"Do you leave for there?"

"We will try," he eyed Phrynus. "This is your concern, how?"

Phrynus raised the bronze hand. "He did this to me."

"At Myonnesus?"

Phrynus nodded.

"I was there," Teutiaplas said, "I was one of Alcidas' captains. He turned out a poltroon," he gestured at Phrynus' hand, "so I left him to aid Paches." He paused. "I am sorry for your hand. Had I known his intentions, I would have intervened."

"That you are here speaks of your honor," Phrynus said, "so, on that honor, I ask a favor."

"That is?"

"Take me on your fleet."

Teutiaplas was appropriately startled. "You cannot row."

"I can." Phrynus fetched an oar and locked it in the hand. Several gathered to watch as he stood on a piling and commanded the oar. "You make odd movements," Teutiaplas observed.

"It's how I keep the hand tight to the oar, by shifting the cords."

Teutiaplas shook his head, "It's unnatural. You'll throw the other rowers off rhythm."

"I will not."

Teutiaplas said nothing and Phrynus saw the rejection. "I must find Alcidas."

"Why?"

Phrynus merely looked at his bronze hand. Teutiaplas frowned. "You'd visit the same on him? Vengeance, citizen? That way is madness."

"But it is a way."

Teutiaplas regarded him. "Paches is not here. He's in Mytilene, attending to business. We go to Patmos after we have offloaded the slaves and cargo and cleaned the remaining ships. You may help with that. It may you will earn passage. It may the hard work burn out your rage, too. Three obols a day."

"The standard is a drachma."

"But you can only do half the work."

Phrynus stilled. He was a practical man and accepted circumstance, no matter how unjustly brought− a headwind preventing landfall, a spoiled cargo− the Fates that reduced expected wages. He recovered from such circumstance through his own efforts, not wailing to the gods, and had earned enough respect for that to ensure future berths. It'd be the same now. "If I show that not to be true, will you adjust my pay?"

"I will."

He was assigned to a gang unloading Mytilene loot from one of Paches' triremes. When emptied, the ship would be stripped and scoured and refitted. A week they had, so the foreman, Erabulus, shrugged and threw Phrynus on the ropes. If Teutiaplas was reduced to hiring cripples, he was not one to question. The other dockmen stared at the bronze-handed man and gave him room should the bad luck clinging to him rub off like the recent plague. Phrynus pulled and hauled and eventually convinced them he would not be a hindrance.

"Move off there!" Erabulus called to the gang sometime after the noon meal and Phrynus joined them at the other side of the cleaning dock. "What's going on?" he asked a caulker, who shrugged, "They bring out the last of the treasures." Must be valuable, indeed, to get them to stand aside, and Phrynus used his bronze hand to ward a place up front. Guards stood on the dock while an official escorted two beautiful women, dressed in house cloth, down the plank into the midst of the soldiers, who arrayed about them protectively and marched away. Must be Paches' household, Phrynus concluded and, impatiently, waited to see what else offloaded. But Erabulus yelled, "Back to it!" and the men, sullen, flowed to their places. Phrynus stopped the caulker, "I thought there was treasure."

"You just saw it."

"What?"

The caulker spat and made a sign invoking luck, "Those two women, Helenais and Lemaxis. Paches had their husbands killed on Mytilene and took them for himself."

Phrynus, shocked, said "That is an evil thing."

"It is," the caulker said and spat once more and invoked more luck and joined the gang. Phrynus did, too, stationing himself at the strongest rope to ease the trireme down into the depths.

The day longed and Phrynus was in the numb state that served him well as a rower, where thought and pain gave way to the rhythm. It was the same at the end of an oar or rope and Phrynus heard, in his stupor, the sounds of grudging admiration from the gang. That drachma would be his by the end of the week.

It turned out sooner. "To me!" Teutiaplas called and the gang formed about the pilot, who was standing on a crate and holding a parchment. "Men of the docks," he said, "we have need of that trireme now."

Erabulus was astonished, "But, pilot, it has just been settled in the bottom mud!"

"I know," Teutiaplas agreed, "but still."

"It has to be scraped and sealed." The impossibility was evident. Even counting the time for the seawater to clean the decks, there were the tasks just named.

"I know," Teutiaplas, sympathetic, "but she is the fastest of the fleet and for this order," he rattled the parchment, "we need all speed."

Erabulus folded his arms. "Three days," he said.

Teutiaplas frowned, ready to argue, but Phrynus stepped forward. "One," he said.

A collective gasp. Teutiaplas stared at him in astonishment while Erabulus did so in rage. "For two drachmas per worker," another collective gasp and Erabulus went purple, "with five for him," Phrynus pointed at the foreman, who was greatly mollified by that. "And one," Phrynus tapped his chest with the bronze hand, "for me."

Everyone held their breath. Teutiaplas gazed at the sun's reach for the west and pointed at it. "By this time tomorrow?"

"Yes," Phrynus said.

"Done."

The gang all looked at Phrynus and then at each other and, with a roar, rushed back to the dock, Erabulus shouting orders. "You get me five drachmas for this," he pushed his face into Phrynus', "and I will cut a dove for your hand at Hephaestus' shrine." Phrynus grinned and found a place on a rope, the men gladly allowing him slack to wind it about his stump.

All through the night, a frenzy of hauling and scouring, the caulkers pouring new oakum while Phrynus and the others ranged the trireme peeling off barnacles and blading the lower decks free of what human waste the seawater missed. By noon, the trireme was on its final side with hot tar running across it and, by midafternoon, it was painted and refitted. By the time Teutiaplas remounted his crate and measured the sun, they were pulling the trireme into its lock. As the last cable was cinched in place, Teutiaplas stepped off the crate and boarded, while the men fell down, almost dead, at their stations. Some time later, Teutiaplas emerged and stepped to the prow where he could see over the exhausted, panting, now mostly asleep, crew. "It is ready," he said, admiration deep in his eyes. The men only grinned at each other, too beat to even cheer, but many at least slapped Phrynus on the shoulder, some touching his bronze hand in reverence.

"Make way," Teutiaplas called and the crew dragged themselves to the other side of the dock. Royal thranites, holding their polished and gleaming oars aloft, marched in phalanx step down to the gangplank. Their eyes remained aloof, ignoring the gang of wharf rats strewn about the dock panting and, watching with envy. Just as well; Phrynus did not want to be recognized. He knew most of them, and didn't want tales of his fall spread about the fleet.

"All thranites?" the caulker whispered. "For all three decks?"

"They must want great speed," Phrynus whispered back. "Why?" the caulker was perplexed. "What's so important?" Phrynus gestured to the middle of the parade, where a messenger, in the whitest of tunics, held before him a gold parchment box. "The message being delivered."

"It is an execution order," Teutiaplas, who was close enough to hear them, said, without turning around. "The Assembly wants all the males of Mytilene dead." Some of the crew gasped at that.

Phrynus did not. He stared at his bronze hand. "Good."

Teutiaplas looked at him, "Vengeance, rower, is a never ending storm."

Phrynus spat. "They're backing Sparta, aren't they?"

Teutiaplas said nothing as the royal crew took possession of the trireme and prepared. Phrynus' arms ached with memory as the oars, in precision, rose, disappeared, then reappeared through the locks in unison. Call from the master and the first stroke, over half on time, backed the trireme out. Phrynus was impressed. "They are very good."

"Cleon's own," Teutiaplas said unnecessarily because Phrynus knew the livery. He'd tried for that stable but he wasn't quite the rower as these. He looked at his hand. Now, he'd never be.

"You've all done a magnificent thing," Teutiaplas announced and began walking down the prostrate crew, shaking some awake to pay them. Erabulus grinned as the five coins dropped into his purse. "I want him with me all the time," he said, pointing at Phrynus, "as a full paid dockman." Teutiaplas agreed, dropping two coins, not one, on Phrynus' lap. Phrynus held them, gratitude showing on his face. He would not starve. Hestia would not lose her home.

"Be here tomorrow," Teutiaplas said and walked away and the crew, those who had not passed out, made their various ways off the dock. Phrynus went home, placing the coins on the table and then curled up on his couch, barely registering Hestia's weeping of relief.

He was up at cockcrow. "Where are you going?" Hestia was preparing cakes from the flour the coins had gotten her last night. "I am now employed," he said, tightening the straps of the hand, "as a porter and fitter." She began to weep, as did the children who envisioned again the ridicule at their lowered status. Phrynus stared at them and pointed his bronze hand at the cakes. "You will eat. You will have a place to sleep. And you can proudly say," this for the children, "that your metal-handed father does twice the work of fleshed ones." And he left, appreciating Zeus' struggles with Hera a bit more.

He was at the dock as the sun fulled and walked up to Erabulus, who laughed and assigned him to a rope detail. They had three triremes to unload, sign of Alcidas' absence from the trade routes and Phrynus asked one of the merchantmen if they had news of the Spartan butcher. "Somewhere off Patmos," the Thracian shrugged, looking at Phrynus' bronze hand with distaste. So, nothing new. "Who pursues him?" Phrynus pressed but the Thracian walked away.

Teutiaplas, who was standing close by, frowned but said nothing.

A flurry and bustling at the top of the pier and everyone stopped. Another contingent stood there, a tall, angry man standing in their middle. "Cleon!" a roper exclaimed and Phrynus stared at the strategos. Why would he be here?

They soon found out. "I need rowers!" the red-faced madman bellowed, the force of his voice almost knocking them to the wharf.

Teutiaplas bowed and spoke softly, "There are none here, strategos. These are all wharfmen."

"They'll do," Cleon glowered at him. "I don't need thranites, just a couple of dozen thalamites to fill the benches." Cleon's voice rose to its typical raging level as he walked into the midst of the astonished workers. "I will pay my standard rate of two drachmas a day!"

A gasp and a rush on Cleon as the wharfmen fought for position. Even Erabulus was in there, no doubt thinking what a lucrative few days this had become. Phrynus snorted because Cleon paid his crew a talent for each voyage and, when everything was settled, the average was considerably more than two drachmas. Cleon was getting a bargain. But what was this? Cleon had dispatched his best crew on the best ship just yesterday.

Odder, Cleon was bypassing the most obviously fit wharfmen for older, spindlier, more broken-down ones. "You, you, you," he pointed through the gang, ignoring the quite healthy Erabulus, which confused the foreman. Cleon almost missed Phrynus then caught the gleam of his bronze hand in the morning light. He stared at it. "Can you row with that thing?"

"Yes," he said guardedly, giving Teutiaplas a warning look.

Cleon smiled. "You, too," and there was a strange light of triumph in his eyes that made Phrynus suspicious. But, a trireme! He stepped into line with the old men, the soaring relief and sense of return balancing out his concerns.

Teutiaplas eyed the selected crew and the grinning Cleon and voiced his own suspicion, "There are better men, strategos." The strangeness of the picks offset Teutiaplas' relief that those better men were left to him.

"They'll do," Cleon repeated and turned to his newly assembled crew. "Athenians!" he announced, "I need your best time and effort to overtake the trireme that left yesterday for Mytilene!"

All of them should have burst out laughing at the sheer ridiculousness. A day's head start and the best crew on the Greek Sea? Sure. But Cleon's murderous eyes kept them silent. "I have another order," he flourished a parchment, "that offsets the one sent yesterday."

The gang looked puzzled but it came clear to Phrynus and, by his cleared brow, Teutiaplas. Of course. The Assembly had suffered a pang of conscience over their murder decree, so they ordered Cleon to countermand it. And he would go through the motions, even to the point of committing the remainder of his livery to the effort. If they didn't quite get there in time, well, too bad, it was the manpower shortage that forced Cleon to use untrained and unskilled thalamites, including a one handed rower, for Zeus' sake.

Phrynus almost smiled. It was masterful, typical of the duplicitous Cleon. And Phrynus gets on a crew and back into his profession…

… until the general ridicule of the failed mission became legend, and then he would never be allowed to look at a trireme, much less crew one. In his mind, Phrynus saw Alcidas slipping out of his grasp.

"Strategos!" he called out. Cleon, already tending to details with Teutiaplas, turned, frowning. "Yes?"

"If we are able to do such a feat," Phrynus began, and here Cleon almost laughed out loud, "will you not reward us?"

The newly hired crew leaned forward eagerly and Cleon looked at them shrewdly. "If you are able to overtake the first order," Cleon could not keep the mirth out of his voice, "what would you want?"

Phrynus made sure to raise his bronzed hand to Cleon's view, "A crew talent." Your standard rate, Cleon.

The crew gasped and made swift calculations and realized how much more was involved and looked at Cleon eagerly. Teutiaplas whispered in Cleon's ear and the strategos peered at Phrynus. "Yes," he said after a moment, "yes, now I recognize you." Phrynus waited. He had banked on that, could almost see Cleon's swift thought—do you see how I tried, Assembly? I even hired a newly unemployed rower, a good one! That he was bronze-handed had nothing to do with it.

It only took a moment. "Done!" Cleon called and the crew cheered and scattered to make ready. Cleon smirked at Phrynus and turned away. He did not see Phrynus smirk back.

Quick arrangements and a harbor crew brought up a trireme. Phrynus frowned at it. Older, heavier by the keel, lots of dipping and the wind would be a problem. Okay, so, the first stroke would have to be a dig and a pull-up, followed by a swift skimming row, one two, one two, like that. "Listen to me," Phrynus said quietly to the others, and he explained the method. One of the oldest stared at him, round eyed, "You can show us?"

"Yes, after we are underway. But don't reveal what you know. And, when we start, be as clumsy as you can."

"I don't think that will be difficult," the oldster laughed and the crew joined in. "Will we win the talent?"

"Yes, if you follow my lead."

"But the other trireme…"

"The problem with elite crews," Phrynus whispered so Cleon couldn't hear, "is their ego." The oldster nodded, understanding. An elite crew fights among themselves, slowing down the ship. Phrynus should know: he'd engaged in such fights with great enthusiasm.

"Load!" Cleon called and Phrynus led the way on board and down the ladders to the lowest level. He quietly showed everyone how to sit, what angle to hold the oars, how to move their feet. Phrynus took a middle lock so he could control the maximum number of thalamites. The oldster slipped in next to him, "I think I'll row with you," he said, grinning, "You have a lucky hand."

"You may not like it," Phrynus warned, "I have to make wild adjustments and I will bump you."

"Then bump me," the oldster shrugged, "just do it with the bronze hand."

Phrynus laughed. The oldster introduced himself, "Carpides," and Phrynus helped him adjust.

"Zygites!" a voice called from outside and Phrynus watched between the boards as the next level up marched on and took position. They looked competent.

"Hey!" there was a shout and a scrambling and Phrynus looked across the row. A couple of the crewmen was scrambling out of a urine stream coming from the zygites above. That amused the rest of the zygites and they added their own streams, which Phrynus expertly dodged. "Is this normal?" Carpides said, wiping his face, not being so expert a dodger.

Phrynus nodded, "And worse to come." Carpides rolled his eyes, realizing what Phrynus meant. "But, they'll get it from the thranites above them."

"Which means we will, too," Carpides muttered.

Phrynus chuckled. "That's why you want to be a thranite."

"Phrynus!" a voice called from the zygite level and he peered up into a pair of mocking eyes. "Nicon," Phrynus said evenly.

"I see you have come down in the world," Nicon's mockery bellowed through the deck.

"And I see you have not gone up," Phrynus replied, which got several others laughing through the two decks, a baleful look from Nicon, and probably a good defecation on Phrynus' shoulders later.

Worth it.

"Cast! Off!" the master called from the top deck and Phrynus cocked his head to listen. Oars locked and lines tossed and he stood. "Watch me!" he called and slipped his bronze hand down the oar, pushing it level. Everyone followed suit, even the normal thalamites, who realized they were in the presence of a veteran. "Strike!" the master called and Phrynus slid the oar out and down, watching with approval as his charges more or less copied his movements. Phrynus felt their bank of oars hit the water within an acceptable time of the zygites. Carpides was amazed, "How do you know what's going on? I can't even see the water."

"You get a feel for it, the rhythm," Phrynus said and set his oar and began to match the strokes of Nicon above him. Not that he liked the blowhard, but Nicon did know his stuff and had an eye on the thranites, so he'd do as a marker. Phrynus looked over his charges and saw the uncoordinated efforts. "Like this!" he called and led the proper sweep of the oar, the back and forth on the bench.

"My ass!" one of the others groaned and Phrynus smiled. "Yes," he said, "you will get giant ass blisters. But think how much salve your share of the talent will buy." They laughed and joked at that and Carpides said, "Could use a seat cushion." Yes, they could, and Phrynus realized their absence was another Cleon sabotage attempt.

Hiring Phrynus, though, was probably the better attempt. Phrynus quickly discovered the bronze hand and its tack required a lot more adjustment then he originally thought and he was throwing Carpides way off rhythm, which, in turn, threw off the opposite bank. Some of the zygites began to snicker at him and he saw Nicon's mocking eye through the plank. "Carpides," Phrynus said, "plant your shoulder against mine, and match my movements. It will be uncomfortable, but we will synch and we can get the whole bank in order."

"I'm used to discomfort," Carpides said and latched onto Phrynus' left side. After a moment, the whole bank was in stroke and Nicon's mocking turned to anger. "Think you can follow?" he yelled and sped up, as did his deck, but Phrynus coolly picked it up and translated it down the row. He smiled at Nicon "Yes, yes we can."

"What's going on down there?" the pilot yelled, "Stay with the count!" Irritably, Nicon returned to the Master's call and, soon, all three banks were in synch. Good.

But only for a moment. Phrynus counted the strokes and frowned. They were slightly off sea pace and he knew, instantly, what was going on.

Cleon had ordered the Master to a less than optimal count. No one would complain; it was an easy enough rhythm that wouldn't tire too much while giving the illusion of speed. If they happened to get there a day late, well, it wasn't for lack of trying, was it? Cleon gets his way. And saves a talent. Phrynus couldn't allow that.

Subtly, he pulled a second ahead. Carpides caught up and then the whole bank did and they were now outstripping the zygites. Phrynus watched them carefully, saw Nicon and the others exchange glances then pick it up a bit. Quickly enough, the thranites did, too.

"Stay with the count!" roared the Master and everyone dropped back. Damn, he was good. Needed another tactic.

"We are better!" Phrynus sang out, and the thalamites all chuckled. Nicon glared at him, "If you were better, you'd be up here!"

"We are better," Phrynus insisted, "we can outstroke any count you make."

"Ha!" Nicon and the others laughed and one of them deliberately aimed a piss stream at an unfortunate thalamite on the other side. "A cripple and a bunch of ancient wharf rats! I think not!"

"Want to bet?"

Nicon blinked, "A bet?" and he looked among his fellows, the shared avarice lighting their eyes. "How much?"

"Deck portion of the talent."

Everyone gasped, the zygites in astonishment, the thalamites in dismay. Whoever lost was essentially working for free.

Carpides stared at him. "What are you doing?" he whispered. "Bear with me," Phrynus whispered back, and then called out to Nicon, "Well?"

"Sure you didn't get a bronze heart along with that hand?" Nicon insulted Phrynus' intelligence and the zygites laughed. "You are crazy, one hand."

"What's the matter, afraid?" Phrynus sneered, "we are, after all, wharf rats and bronze handed."

Nicon gritted his teeth and Phrynus felt it, the sudden lurch in speed. "With me!" he called to the thalamites and paced and felt the zygites pick up another stroke so he adjusted and they were in rhythm and the thranites matched…

… and they were flying across the water.

"Get back on the count!" the Master called down.

"Jump over the side!" yelled Nicon and all three decks roared with laughter and bent to it and the Master had lost control of the ship. Happened before. And if a Master didn't want to end up swimming home, he went along.

"You're a genius," Carpides puffed.

"We'll see," Phrynus replied grimly, because the effort was already showing. The cords cut into his shoulder and side and his arm went numb and he could see the gasping mouths and pooling sweat of his charges. They'd be dead in an hour. "Leave yourselves!" he called out. They looked at him in puzzlement. "Like the day and night we spent preparing the first trireme," he reminded, and they knew. Minds emptied, jaws slacked, and they became a mass of scooting, pulling, burning automatons.

And they flew over the water.

Day somehow became night and there was no let up. Phrynus no longer saw the hours but only counted strokes, a part of him watchful for any slowdown; Nicon and the zygites were continually dropping off this punishing pace. Phrynus was, too, but motive trumped exhaustion and he adjusted the count back up, even if it took him a few moments longer to realize the change.

"I. Cannot. Continue!" Carpides gasped between strokes.

"Two. Talents!" Phrynus gasped back and that became their oar song. "Two talents, two talents!" chanted among the thalamites, and the zygites, realizing the implications, also picked it up and soon, the entire ship. Even the Master joined in, no doubt convinced they would not make it, even at this rate, so he would keep his job. And his head.

Dawn came, a gradual lightening and Phrynus was in another place. He had reached oneness with the gods, where his strokes were sacrifice and a gloriously golden Zeus stood above, laughing and showering him with wine. Maybe it was piss and sweat from the zygites, but it didn't feel like it.

"Look!" someone called from the upper deck and that was so startling the oars locked and bumped each other as they all stared out their ports.

On the horizon. Lesbos.

A cheer went through the entire crew, talents lost or won not in consideration. They had broken a record held by a very celebrated ship, one of Pericles', no less. They were now famous. They would be recorded in halls of heroes, their names sung at festival. But they were not there yet.

"To it! To it!" Phrynus choked through cracked lips, pushing at Carpides and the others and soon they were underway, the rising sun silhouetting their target. In hours that were eternal, they rounded the head and were in Mytilene harbor...

...and saw the other trireme, Cleon's best, still off-loading.

A wilder cheer broke out and made their strokes frantic and, impossibly, they picked up speed. The Master roared, "Back off!" because the speed would carry them through the dock and they reversed oars, the sudden lurch throwing Carpides from his seat. Phrynus grabbed the old man's oar to prevent backlash but that took them off line and they made a sloppy entry, the side of the trireme sliding hard against the planking. The piermen at the other trireme stopped, stared, and ran for their lives. But the dock held and the trireme braked, stopping short.

A scurrying from the top deck and Phrynus saw a messenger leap off the side, white toga flying, a parchment held high before him. He ran to the astonished piermen and there was a quick conversation then fingers pointed up a hill. The messenger pelted off.

They had done it.

Phrynus slipped off the bench and folded into the passage, He was unconscious in seconds.

Someone shook his shoulder. "Bronze hand," a voice said gently.

Phrynus opened his eyes. It felt like a Boetian had worked him over with a hammer. His throat was sand and his lips would not part. He couldn't see, either, so, on top of everything he was now blind but, no, no, it was just dark. Evening dark.

"Bronze hand," the voice said again and shook him again.

Phrynus located him. "Carpides," he croaked.

The old man smiled and lifted a skin to Phrynus' lips and he tasted wine. "Don't gulp," Carpides warned as Phrynus did just that, choking himself. The old man patiently offered more and Phrynus regained his senses. He was still in the passage, exactly where he had collapsed.

"Feeling better, bronze hand?" Carpides hovered.

"My name is Phrynus."

"Not anymore." Carpides helped him up and, together, they stumbled across the floor and up the stairs and onto the open deck where the rest of them lay. As soon as he appeared, the crew stood and gave a rousing cheer, lifting him up and bringing him to a stew pot. Hungrily, Phrynus reached for a cup.

"Amazing, just amazing," the Master stood to the side, shaking his head.

"Have we not killed you?" Phrynus, wary, presumed the Master would gut him.

"So you figured it out." The Master's eyes narrowed. "I thought so. But, don't worry about your little revolt there, bronze hand. The fame of it saves me."

Made sense. Even Cleon wouldn't touch a man who had beaten the previous record, no matter how much it cost politically.

"Uh, Phrynus." Nicon shuffled up, looking worried. Phrynus immediately understood why. Nicon and his zygites had just broken a record for free.

Phrynus sipped lamb stew and gathered strength. He looked at Nicon and his worried zygites, the triumphant thalamites, and the impassive thranites, who waited for the inevitable battle. They would throw in where the advantage developed.

"Phrynus," Nicon's voice was a plead, "we won't get paid until we get back. And then you'll take it and we'll have nothing to show."

"Then you shouldn't have bet!" shouted a thalamite and there was a mutter of agreement or rage, depending on whether you stood to gain or not. The battle was moments away.

Phrynus held up his bronze hand. "We are all a talent ahead, aren't we?" Everyone looked at each other and nodded. "Isn't that better than originally hoped?" Another general nodding.

Phrynus pointed at Nicon, "Didn't these worthies help us get it?" Silence as the point sank in. The thalamites looked at each other, frowning. The zygites looked at each other, hopeful. "Then, we all share. We still get our portion of the talent. And we get new brothers. What say you?" this to the thalamites, who took in breaths to protest, then considered. Saying no meant fighting where half of them die and then bad feelings and vendetta follow for years. But say yes, become richer and obtain the chance at additional jobs.

No contest.

"Cheers for bronze hand!" Nicon called at the sense of it and the rest hurrahed and backs were slapped and hands clasped and, yes, there were still hard feelings, but those would be paid later, individually.

"You should be in the Assembly," the Master chuckled as he handed Phrynus a skin of better wine while celebration took over the ship.

"No thanks, want to see an old age," Phrynus said as he took the skin and drank deeply.

"Boat coming," someone called and they all looked. A skiff pulled for them from the opposite side of the harbor. One of the thalamites dropped the ladder and the skiff tied off. Some soldiers came up, followed by officers. In their middle stood a tall man, imperious, robe pulled tight, armour on but helmet off, carried by a lackey.

"Paches." The Master bowed low, and they all followed suit.

The admiral looked them over. "I understand that you have established a new record."

The Master bowed again. "We have."

Paches regarded him sourly. "Then you have saved me from a grave error. The execution order against the Mytilenes has been stayed. Although," Paches smiled without humor, "there will be reparations of a sort." He blinked at the Master. "You are to be congratulated. And rewarded."

The words did not match the look, and Phrynus wondered at the disconnect. He seemed to be the only one noting it, though, as the crew jumped eagerly at the idea of more treasure. The

Master smiled greedily and looked up, his eyes falling on Phrynus. He hesitated. He could take full credit, but the mood of the crew and Phrynus' sudden popularity might undo him. Phrynus saw the instant calculations in the Master's eyes and almost smiled when he said, "It was not all my doing, admiral. One of our thalamites helped spur us."

"A thalamite?" Paches was taken back. "Who?"

The Master gestured and the crew parted until Phrynus stood apart in their middle. Paches gazed at him. "You have a bronze hand," he said wonderingly as the torchlight sparkled on it.

"I do." Phrynus held it up. "In the service of Athens, admiral."

"Was it service to Athens that prompted your effort, thalamite, or service to Plutus?" Paches grinned, again humorless, and Phrynus felt the insult. So did the others, who started a bit. "We have earned a talent, General, that it is true," he said, dryly, "and other rewards to be determined, all well-deserved." The crew murmured in agreement. "But I seek Alcidas."

"Alcidas?" Paches' brow furrowed. "He is making his cowardly way down the coast. He was spotted off Clarus."

Phrynus nodded. "Fleeing for home. Do you pursue?"

"I do not. I am recalled." And he stared at Phrynus, something unreadable on his face.

Puzzling. Who would recall such an effective soldier? Something stirred, the memory of the two women off-loading and the words of the caulker and his own reaction. It came clear. Paches was called to account, and it probably wouldn't go well for him. There were still Mytilene sympathizers in Athens. No wonder his face offset his words.

"Eurymedon here," Paches gestured at another officer, who stepped up, "is going after the Spartans, though."

Eurymedon was smaller, darker, looked almost Persian. "What is your business with Alcidas?" he asked Phrynus.

Phrynus waggled the hand. Eurymedon stared. " Myonnesus?"

No need to respond.

Eurymedon and Paches exchanged looks. "You mean," Paches said, "you spurred this crew to these efforts because you thought I was attending Alcidas?"

"Yes."

Paches was speechless for a moment, then burst out laughing, real humor this time. "By Zeus." He wiped his eyes. "The Furies settle on this one and I am undone. The gods and their surrogates," and he shook his head.

The crew muttered at that and moved away from Phrynus, making the signs against evil. Amazing how quickly one turned from charm to spell. Phrynus, ignoring them, spoke to Eurymedon. "Do you seek Alcidas?"

"I do," the admiral was guarded. "But I am in need of spearmen as well as oarsmen."

Phrynus looked around and saw a lance by one of the benches. He flipped out the inner circle and, hefting the lance, feinted at the ocean. "I can do both," he said.

A murmur of appreciation from the crew but Eurymedon's look did not change. "We are leaving in the morning. You will not have time to get your talent share back in Athens."

No doubt Eurymedon shared Paches' conviction that greed overwhelmed justice. Phrynus glared at the admiral and turned to the Master. "For 1 percent of my share, will you deliver the rest to my lady?"

The Master did not hesitate, "Surely!" He'd be a fool not to. And with so many witnesses, he'd be a fool to cheat.

Phrynus cocked his head at Eurymedon, who shrugged. "All right. You seem to have a black luck about you." He stared pointedly at Paches, "And probably best you not be on the return journey." Paches snorted in agreement, eying Phrynus murderously.

Phrynus gathered his bag and went down the ladder into Eurymedon's launch. He was surprised to find Carpides and Nicon there, too. "What about your talent share?" he asked.

"Made the same arrangements with the Master," Nicon said.

"You've got Hermes' hand on your shoulder. We'll probably double our earnings with you," Carpides piped enthusiastically.

Phrynus chuckled. Eurymedon, who stood nearby, overheard and pointed at the bronze hand. "Are you sure that was a misfortune?"

Phrynus considered. "That one god soothed the abuse of another doesn't absolve Alcidas."

Eurymedon shook his head and stared at Phrynus. "We Greeks savor the vengeance in our hearts," and he turned away.

Wasn't vengeance the spur to justice? Phrynus would have asked that out loud, but no need. Eurymedon was a self-refute. He was gathering a fleet to pursue the Spartan pirate. And there were dead Mytilenians who might contend with the admiral's lofty sentiments.

Besides, Mars was ascendant and the Furies his handmaids, while Fortune reaped and sewed. Phrynus watched as the fleet loomed and soldiers bustled about the flagship to receive the skiff. The play of it stretched before him like a frieze, and he gasped because there was war and blood and drowned ships across the Greek Sea, even to the colonies. Years and years, all lost, ending in a blur in a great harbor.

"Are you all right?" Carpides asked.

Phrynus looked down at his bronze hand glowing in starlight, restless, itching now with lust. "I will be," he said.

NOTE: On the lists of Athenian
dead from the battles around
Syracuse, are the names Carpides,
Nicon, and Phrynus. That is all we
know.

Pollen

by Ana Manwaring

I think I've landed on Dagobah when we arrive home from our ten days in New Mexico last week. You know, that overgrown planet where Yoda lived in Star Wars? Ok, so I don't actually find any trees growing out of my roof, but it takes a machete to hack a path to the door.—even in the longest drought in California's memory.

Weeds, tall and tangled, sway gently in the breeze over the sprawl of growth hugging the ground.

"What happened to the driveway? Where'd this meadow come from?" I ask my husband in horror, noticing milk thistles, the prickly bane of my garden, already taller than I am. "I could harvest those for liver supplements," I add, eyeing the lifetime supply growing along the carport.

"Late rain," he replies as the Prius bounces over tufts of grass patch-worked with super-sized dandelions and bittercress.

David holds the door while I wrestle my suitcase across the pea gravel. The wheels catch in a tangle of burclover that sprawls across the welcome mat. Was this noxious weed here when we left? I can already see the tender-looking seedpods that will ripen into nasty brown burrs and lodge into everything—my feet, the cat, the carpets.

The sight of this herbaceous splendor causes my eyes to water, my sinuses to clog. And then, "Ah-ah-ah-choo!"

I yank my bag over the jamb. "It's hay-fever season," I lament and slam the door behind me, bolting it against the spring menace.

"Welcome to the Pollen Capital of the World," my allergy-free husband jokes.

I'd have laughed but laughing makes me cough. Sonoma County, with its beautiful expanses of grass and forested hills, is one of the worst places for seasonal allergy sufferers—about a quarter of our population, not counting the dogs. My head pounds and my eyes itch just thinking of the days to come. I read that 70% of the pollen in the air comes from grass and according to a recent article in the AARP Bulletin, grasses and trees are spewing 21% more pollen than 30 years ago, and allergy season starts 20 day earlier now than in 1990 because of the CO_2 in the atmosphere. The late rains and climate warmed air have made my weeds lush, thick, and bursting into pollen-filled flower.

In normal years, whatever that means these days, the grass would have started to bloom late-April and continue through Memorial Day, but I've heard tell the misery could continue into July this year. Just thinking about that makes me run to the medicine cabinet for a saline snort off the neti pot.

I unpack my suitcase into the laundry and empty the contents of my cosmetics bag back into the bathroom—shampoo, toothpaste, aspirin, razor blades. I'd forgotten to pack my antihistamines for the trip and I hadn't missed them. Two weeks of New Mexico desert, tumbling tumbleweeds, junipers and sagebrush, and nary a sneeze. Was it the craft beer, I wonder as I slip the bottle of Dark Ops—thankfully intact—out of my bag.

I give my theory a test. The first medicinal sip of the smooth chocolate bitterness soothes my scratchy throat. My headache disappears with the next. This stuff really works! I'm ready to brave the outdoors and visit my California native garden: ceanothus, monkey flower, Cleveland sage and poppies all in bloom. But the bed is so choked by non-native grasses, bristly ox tongue, and sow thistles going to seed that I can't see my beautiful flowers, not even the taller gooseberries and wild currants.

The oaks and willows, which crowd the banks of our creek, are in pollen-spewing flower, adding to the miasma of allergens in the air. I can see the pollen blowin' in the wind, a yellowish particulate smudge. Next it will be the olives, emitting more pollen into my atmosphere. I shoot my little orchard a dirty look.

"Ah-choo. Ah-Choo. AH-CHOO." My head feels like it's exploded. Maybe another shot of Dark Ops will help. I flee back into the house.

"More beer?" David asks.

I've got my hand on the bottle, but release my grip. He's right. Instead, I'll take a shower and make a cup of hot tea with the Tolay Star Thistle honey a friend gave me. The pollen in this local honey is reputed to help minimize the effects of our local allergens.

I sit in my living room, sipping my honeyed tea, watching weed seed float across the yard on the breeze. My sinuses cleared up in the shower's steam and I feel good. Outside the window, a tiny breeze riffles through the tops of silvery eucalyptus, and the green, green grass running up Sonoma Mountain bobs its bloomin' seed heads, welcoming me home.

Scoop

by Guy Thair

Geoff

Geoff Standish stared down at the keyboard in irritation, then back up at the pristine white screen of his computer, willing his brain to come up with a new angle. His stomach rumbled loudly and looked at his watch, noticing he'd missed his break and wondering if he could sneak out before his boss returned from yet another extended, boozy lunch

He hadn't appreciated how easy he'd had it, when he'd been chief writer on the tiny local paper at home and, until he started as junior crime correspondent on the Evening Echo, it hadn't occurred to him how difficult it would be to make his name; now he had to compete for stories with Darren, the ambitious young reporter who ran the crime desk.

It wasn't that Geoff was a bad writer, exactly, but he had done a fair amount of blagging at the interview to secure this, the next step on the road to his dream job of reporting for the nationals. He knew it had been a risk, lying about his qualifications, but he had figured his resumé would be enough to convince any new employer of his suitability for the position; especially since the editor at his last paper was his ex father-in-law and Geoff had reckoned on a getting a good reference from him, even if it was just to make sure he left the paper and didn't come back.

Splitting up with Mandy had obviously been a factor in him changing jobs, but he managed to persuade himself that he'd finally made the move to the big time because he had outgrown the parochial little rag he'd worked for since leaving school (conveniently ignoring the fact that Mandy's father and two brothers had promised to beat the shit out of him if he ever spoke to her again) and, despite everyone else knowing his ex-wife had taken his job like the opportunistic bitch she was, he knew his destiny as a Pulitzer prize winning journalist was still within reach

The trouble was, there wasn't a lot to report on around here and he had been reduced to writing a weekly "around the courts" column, which was no more than a list of neighbourhood drunks, vandals and bored teenagers, fighting in the city centre on a Saturday night.

What he needed was a proper crime, something he could really get his teeth into.

Mandy

She drained the last mouthful of cheap coffee, dropped her paper cup into the bin with an expression of distaste and glared around the empty office. Why had she taken this bloody dead end job in the first place? If she hadn't been so keen to fuck Geoff over, she never would have accepted her father's offer to "make a bit of extra spending money", particularly if she'd known how much of her time it would take up.

What was even worse, that useless little turd had got himself a proper job with a big city paper, which he wouldn't have had the guts to apply for if it hadn't been for the family cutting him loose when they divorced last year. She didn't know why her father hadn't cut out the middleman and sent her to the Echo with a glowing reference, and simply sacked her idiot ex-husband.

Except of course, she did know; alimony. If Geoff was out of work, she wouldn't get the money her father's flash lawyer had managed to screw out of him in the divorce.

She was almost disappointed that he hadn't tried to get in touch with her since they split up, if only because of the kicking her bothers would happily inflict on him if he dared come around here again…

All of a sudden Mandy became very still and for a while she appeared deep in thought.

After a minute or two, she began to smile.

Darren

"Fuck!"

Darren Blake wasn't having a good day.

"You bastards, I'll sue you to fucking smithereens, you wait and see!"

He stood on the kerb, shaking his fist at the recovery vehicle as it towed his brand new Porsche away from the restaurant, the bright yellow clamp easily visible against the gleaming black paintwork.

He'd only had a quick working lunch and a couple of drinks, he couldn't have been more than half an hour over on the parking meter, 45 minutes, tops. And when he came out, those two fucking gorillas in hi-vis jackets were winching his beloved car onto their bloody flatbed truck like it was some piece of scrap to be junked. Well, if they'd as much as scuffed the tyres, he'd have their bollocks for desk ornaments.

Darren smiled grimly, "bollocks for desk ornaments", that was a good one, he'd have to remember that, for when he was recounting the story of this shitty day to the lads in the office…he looked at his watch; "Shit." Darren looked up and down the busy street, "Taxi!"

Geoff

Geoff had just finished the last of his court reports; a case involving a dispute over the height of a conifer hedge, a story not even the most sensationalist reporter could make interesting, when the sound of a phone ringing made him look up. It wasn't his phone, he hardly ever got calls from outside lines this late on a Friday afternoon, so he stood up to look over his cubicle and saw a light flashing on Darren's fancy desk console.

Should he answer it? It could be a huge story, he'd kick himself if he missed his big break through indecisiveness at a time like this.

He stared at the light, flashing in time with the phone's insistent ringing, sounding loud in the deserted office.

"Oh, what the hell."

He walked quickly round the partition, proud of his ability to make snap decisions, and snatched up the receiver in a way that he (wrongly) thought of as being the way a go-getting, thrusting young executive answered the phone. Sadly, the cord was a lot shorter than he'd realised and the receiver sprang out of his hand and clattered against the side of the desk before Geoff got it anywhere near his ear.

"Oh, for fuck's sake."

He was just bending down to retrieve the dangling phone handset, from which he could hear the tinny "Hello...hello?..." of the caller's voice, when a voice a lot closer to home made Geoff grit his teeth and groan inwardly.

"Whoa there, Geoff! You taking up phone juggling? Hahaha!"

He looked up to see Darren, striding in through the double doors of the office, like he was making a grand entrance at a fucking state dinner, shrugging out of his poncey camel hair coat and peeling off those ridiculous fucking driving gloves he insisted on wearing, (he would have been even more furious if he'd known Darren had arrived by cab) then reaching out an imperious hand for the phone as Geoff finally managed to wrestle it into submission.

"Fuck you, Darren, I got to it first. Who the fuck do you think you are anyway? Swanning around like you fucking own the place, you're not fit to shine my shoes, you piece of shit..."

...Is what Geoff wanted to say.

But instead, he just meekly handed the phone to his smirking boss and scuttled back to his cubicle, seething with self-hatred and, more importantly, Darren-hatred, as he listened to the one sided conversation.

"Hello, sorry about that, my assistant is rather clumsy today."…..(Geoff could feel a vein in his temple throbbing)…"Yes, yes this is the crime desk, Darren Blake speaking, how may I help you?"….."Oh, hi Stacey love, I thought I recognized that sexy voice, haha, what have you got for me?"….."Really? And where was this?"……"You're a star, Stacey, haven't I always said so?"……"Hahaha, oooh, you'll get me into trouble one of these days, you little minx. Let me buy you dinner one night, ok?"….."Mmm, I'd love to. I'll speak to you soon, gotta go babe, call me. Ciao Bella, mwah!"

Darren glanced over at Geoff's cubicle, from where there came a sharp splintering noise and some muffled swearing. He frowned and snapped his fingers loudly a few times, as if summoning a particularly inattentive waiter.

"Geoff?" **snap snap** "Geoff, I need to borrow your car, mate." **snap snap** "Come on, keys, I'm in a hurry."

Geoff paused in the act of picking splinters of the pencil he'd been holding out of the palm of his hand and slowly rose from his chair, peering suspiciously over the partition at Darren, still holding his hand out impatiently.

"Come on, come on, I haven't got all day." **snap snap** "That was my police contact, with a tip about a robbery over in Thornbury. I'm going over there to interview the alleged victim now and my motor has been fucking clamped, so I need yours."

"Umm, but I was…"

"Yeah, well you'll have to get the bus home, won't you? This is a big story, I'm not losing out to some hack from the nationals, just because you got all precious about your bloody Citroen Picasso."

Geoff hesitated, maybe he could reach some sort of compromise?

"How about if I drive you?" He fished the keys out of his pocket, but stopped short of handing them over.

"Nah, sorry Geoff, this is strictly need to know, old chap," Darren took a quick step forward and snatched the keys before he had a chance to react, "confidential informants and all that, you know how it is."

He turned to go, the camel coat flaring out dramatically from his shoulders as he pocketed Geoff's keys, then as an afterthought, he looked back with a grin.

"Don't forget to keep your bus ticket, you can put in a claim for travel expenses, hahaha."

Then he was gone and Geoff was alone in the office once more.

Stacey

Stacey grinned to herself as she hung up the phone. She didn't know what sort of prank her friend Mandy was pulling on that twat, Darren from the Echo, but whatever it was, he deserved it. "Ciao Bella" ? Really? What a prick.

Geoff

Geoff stepped through the front doors of the Evening Echo building and turned up the collar of his jacket against the drizzle, just in time to see his own car pull away from its parking space and head for the main exit. A taxi pulled up and four girls from the typing pool got out and pushed past him without even glancing in his direction, chattering and laughing together, completely unaware of his existence. He glared bitterly at their retreating figures, despising them for their happiness, turned back to the cab, then looked once more for his car and saw it was just pulling out into traffic.

Then, on the spur of the moment, feeling like a real investigative journalist for a change, he yanked open the taxi's rear door, jumped in and held a twenty pound note over the seat to the startled driver.

"Follow that car!"

Mandy

Mandy stood at the window, smoking nervously and watching the gated entrance of her gravel driveway for the arrival of her guest. She was confident the call to her friend at the police station would make her pathetic excuse for an ex-husband come running, hungry for The Big Story that would make his career, and she didn't want to miss the start of the show.

She didn't have long to wait. Mandy was stubbing out her cigarette in an overflowing ashtray when she saw a car swing into the drive. The rain, falling more heavily now, was visible in the headlight beams as late afternoon turned to dusk and dusk, in turn, lost its battle with the gathering storm clouds, the resulting gloom filtering everything through a grey murk that reduced visibility to a few yards.

Geoff's Citroen pulled up by the front door and Mandy frowned in irritation as he parked the wrong way round, brake lights flaring briefly through the rain. The interior light came on, she saw his silhouette lean across the seat to grab something and a few seconds later he climbed out, shrugged into that grotty old raincoat of his and hurried to reach the shelter of the porch.

Darren

Darren flipped the wipers on as the drizzle turned to a steady downpour and peered through the windscreen, trying to make out road signs as he passed yet another narrow junction on the unlit country lane.

"Bloody hell, Geoff, haven't you ever heard of SatNav, for fuck's sake?"

He glanced down at the open notebook on the seat next to him, checking the address once more and looked up just in time to see he was approaching a crossroads. He slowed Geoff's car to be sure he didn't miss anything, scanning the signpost on the corner,

"Barnfield Road, yes! Thank fuck for that."

Darren turned left and continued for another half a mile before he saw lights ahead of him, which as he got closer he realised were attached to gate posts. This looks like the place, he thought, pulling into the gateway and driving up to the large, ivy-covered house, where he parked and looked up in distaste at the shitty weather outside. Not wanting to get his expensive coat soaking wet, he took one of Geoff's that he'd found on the back seat, picked up his notebook and stepped out into the rain.

Turning the collar up, he ran to the front door and had his foot on the first of three wide stone steps when he was grabbed violently from behind and a heavy sack was thrown over his head. Darren tried to yell for help, but a punch to the kidneys knocked the wind out of him. While he was gasping for air something was pulled roughly across his mouth, his head was yanked back as the coarse material of the sacking cut into his face and tongue and he gagged.

His attacker was not only unseen, but also silent, emitting only the occasional grunt as he easily held onto the struggling crime reporter, but then he heard another voice, shockingly close to his right ear.

"Hello, Geoff, looks like you've been a naughty boy, coming round here where you're not wanted."

The owner of the voice tutted, as if this was a personal disappointment to him and that Geoff had badly let him down.

"Except I'm not fucking Geoff!" Darren wanted to scream, but he couldn't make anything more than choking, wheezing noises, so he just frantically shook his head and prayed this was all some kind of horrible mistake.

Then he heard a door open somewhere in front of him and a woman's voice spoke to whoever held him.

"Take him into the barn, we don't want a mess in the house."

His captor's grip loosened as he switched hands for a brief second and Darren broke free and made a run for it. He desperately sprinted away from the voices, only half-registering the sound of laughter, thinking he had to be heading away from the house and towards the road.

He thought that for about five seconds, because after that he ran into the side of Geoff's car.

Hard.

Geoff

Geoff, meanwhile, was crouched in the shadow of a dripping conifer hedge halfway down the drive, having successfully tailed his own car in a taxi all the way to…Mandy's house!

He couldn't fucking believe it, how did Darren not know whose house this was? Her old man was in newspapers, for fuck's sake, he attended all the press piss-ups and had even visited The Echo once as a guest of their chief executive. Some bloody crime editor he is, Geoff thought bitterly, I could do his job standing on my head.

He watched as Darren climbed out of his car and scurried to the front door.

"That's my coat, you thieving…"

Then Geoff saw Mandy's two brothers; a couple of gorillas in jogging suits, jumping out of the flower beds that surrounded the area in front of the house and grabbing Darren as he got to door of the porch. One of them dropped a hood over his head and gagged him, before the door opened and his ex-wife appeared.

After Darren's abortive escape attempt had left him unconscious on the immaculate gravel, Geoff watched in horror as the gorilla twins dragged his limp body round the side of the house and into the darkened barn. A few minutes later, Mandy came out of the house and followed them inside, closing the door behind her.

Mandy

Mandy felt a thrill of excitement as she walked quickly through the rain to the barn; she had been waiting for this for too long not make the most of it and now it was actually happening, she wanted to savour every minute.

The door swung closed behind her and she headed to the far end of the darkened building where the small tractor and plough was parked under a circle of yellow light, cast by a single shaded bulb. It also illuminated the sad figure of Geoff, who was tied to a wooden chair, sack over his head and rope gag still in place. Mandy saw with amusement that he hadn't got rid of that horrible old coat, which must be all of ten years old by now, but then Geoff never had been any good at buying clothes, as she had constantly pointed out to him, to no avail.

Her brothers, Derek and Kevin, were standing either side of the chair, looking very pleased with themselves indeed, so she gave them a nod of gratitude as she approached the strange little tableau; like a gangster, about to exact terrible revenge on a rival, she thought, with two of her top wise guys there to back her up.

"So, Geoff, you seem to have got yourself in a spot of bother. Why on Earth would you come round here on a night like this, when you surely knew the kind of welcome you'd get?"

At this, Geoff began to make some very odd noises and started to thrash about in his chair a fair bit, all of which Del and Kev found highly amusing and let him continue for a moment, before Kev gave him a swift back-hander round the side of the head and he toppled over.

Right onto the upturned blade of the tractor's folding plough.

The tip of the sharply pointed blade punched straight through sack, skin and skull as if it were no harder than the clay soil in the fields. The bound figure jerked violently for a couple of seconds, then slumped and hung, shifting with an unpleasant cracking noise as the weight of the body in the chair was preventing from reaching the ground by the steel blade buried in its head.

Mandy stared in horror at the rapidly spreading pool of blood, more pouring from the stained sacking by the second and she tried to scream. Nothing came out except a strangled squeak and her legs buckled under her; she collapsed to her knees on the hard bricks and the last thing she saw before she was swallowed by the black pit of unconsciousness were her two brothers, being noisily sick on each other's feet.

Darren

Eeerrghh, Ow, what the fuck? What the FUCK!? Who was that crazy bitch? And why did she think I was that twat, Geoff, for fuck's sake? I can't fucking move…Wait, I'm fucking tied up!

"Mmmffghff drrg ghrrffff mmnggff!!"

This fucking gag, I'm going to choke, you bastards. What the fuck do they want? Wait, what's that…footsteps? The bitch is back, shit.

"So, Geoff, you seem to have got yourself in a spot of bother…"

I'm not Geoff, you fucking stupid cow! Why don't you understand, whatever you think I've done, I'm not him! Look, just take off this fucking hood and you'll…

Owww, you cu…

Oh shit, I'm falling over, catch me you bastards…

Whooaaaaa…

Crunch.

Geoff

Geoff ran to the door of the barn as soon as it closed behind Mandy and peered in through a knot hole. He watched events unfold, clapping a hand over his mouth to stop his cry of horror giving him away as Darren met his sudden demise, then turned and half ran, half stumbled to his car. With a sigh of relief he saw Darren had left the keys in the ignition and he simply got in and drove away.

When he was a safe distance from the house, Geoff pulled over and rested his head on the steering wheel for a moment, until he got the shaking under control. Then he made two phone calls; an anonymous one to the police and another, slightly more satisfying one to his editor, who he interrupted while he was at a press association dinner.

"This had better be bloody good, Standish, they're just bringing out the brandy. Have you finally found your Big Story, you bloody well better have?"

"Yes sir," said Geoff, staring out into the rainy night, "I think you could say that, yes

The Fishing Quarter

• • ● • •

by Lisa Towles

I thought I smelled smoke coming from my living room in the middle of the night. Walking across cold tiles in bare feet, my eyes felt swollen, and my head was still heavy with the glue of deep slumber. A tiny, orange glow in the pitch-black revealed Gino's presence from six feet away.

"I told you not to smoke in here."

"I needed to see you."

"We agreed on three weeks."

"It's been four weeks, three days, twelve hours —"

I waved my hand in the air. It was always the same with Gino. "I don't necessarily want to be away from you, but I need to be alone."

"Is that why you came to Barceloneta?"

"My father lives here," I said as a lame excuse.

He saw through this. "You haven't said a word to him in almost twenty years. Why do you want to see him now?" he raised his voice and slurred a few syllables, exposing both his flair for drama and his alcohol consumption.

"He sent me a note." It's true, it wasn't a bona fide reason, but nothing I could say to Gino about my father would be acceptable. He not only had heard the family saga but had watched much of it unfold. I could barely understand my connection to Gino, let alone explain it to someone else. But I was a modern woman with old world ideas, and monogamy was as engrained in my programming as was being female. He came home every night, paid his share of the bills and didn't run around. These virtues alone presented an irresistible alternative to the chaos of growing up with Rascal Perez.

He pulled the chain on the lamp beside the wooden chair.

Shielding my eyes from the light, I leaned against the wall. "Rascal needs me now."

"The last time he needed you, you ended up with a black eye."

"I don't need to be reminded."

He stood, all six foot two inches of him, and slammed a glass he had been holding against the marble coffee table. "What makes you want to help him now, for God's sake? You refuse to be with a man who loves you but choose to help one who's treated you like a stray dog all your life. If Rascal thought he could get a fair price, he'd sell you to the damn gypsies."

"I know what he is and I know what he isn't. If you don't understand, then I can't explain it to you."

From the open window behind the couch, a breeze blew through the room and vacuumed up all the stale air and smells leftover from supper. It lifted the bottom of my nightgown a few inches and its cool tongue caressed my bare thighs and belly.

"You're what I don't understand," he said in a gentler voice.

I knew he didn't, and when I looked into his face, I noticed his eyes were red and swollen. When he got drunk enough, Gino could cry if the phone rang. I went to the kitchen and put on a pot of coffee. He didn't move from the living room.

"How did you find me?" I asked him, realizing all the while that anything he said now would have to be edited for content. He was loaded and I had hurt his feelings — recipe for disaster.

"Sonya's son knows Luis from the fruit market. I found him in that bar on the promenade. The Mandolin something."

I smiled. "The Harp and Mandolin. You probably saw Rascal without even knowing it."

"Does he drink there?"

"He owns the place. It was the first thing he did when he got back from the war. He came to Barcelona with a pile of money, God knows where

165

he got it, and bought a little shack in Barceloneta that had a cafe next door."

"It's a sissy name for a cafe."

"Actually he plays the mandolin in a group. They perform down at the waterfront here on Friday nights in a fishing boat with lights on it. People sit on the docks drinking wine with their feet in the water and listen to them."

I heard his heavy footsteps against the wood floors as he followed the aroma of coffee. "How do you know this?" he asked with thickly knitted brows. I poured my strong coffee into two glass mugs and brought a small pitcher of fresh milk to the table. Gino looked up but said nothing. I'd always been able to read his thoughts, but tonight was different. Red, irritated and overtired, he looked as if he could either strangle me or fall asleep any second. In his condition, I would have been safer chumming for sharks.

"I'm all out of sugar," I said and involuntarily smiled, remembering the cold day twenty years ago when I ran out of my apartment with no coat on and borrowed a pound of sugar. This is how adulthood started for me. He was my only neighbor at the time.

With a wounded expression, Gino smirked and loosened the same white necktie he wore every day. He saw my eyes on it.

"Why don't you wear any of the ties I bought you?" I asked with no emotion in my voice. He could tell I didn't care what tie he wore and was just making nervous conversation. I tapped the table with my fingertips.

"I don't like them as much as this one."

"A white tie makes you look like the mafia."

Gino grabbed my hand gently and rubbed it with his fingers. He looked in my eyes and then quickly away.

"I read about your show in the newspaper," he said.

"I was hoping they'd print something about it. Now more people will come."

"Did you have many students this week?"

"Just one or two in the mornings. I've been closing the studio after lunch every day. I'm thinking of taking some time off after the recital."

He pulled his hand away and sipped the coffee, then winced. The wind howled. Another breeze, this time of low tide.

"For how long?" he asked.

"I don't know yet. A few months maybe."

"Everybody's unhappy these days. Depressed, restless, busy every day doing nothing."

"I never said I was unhappy," I shot back. "It's just that I'm 46 now, too old to dance the way I used to or dance the way Flamenco should be done. I don't have the same agility anymore. Besides, Miguel's coming here soon when he graduates, and I don't know. Actually I'm thinking of selling the studio."

"What?"

I got up and started pacing, as was my custom when my thoughts got tangled. Gino had paid half the down payment on the studio, so he had a stake in the matter. Any rash decisions would be unfair. Though I knew this consciously, I also knew the artistic agony of creative burnout. I was already there. "Rascal's sick, Gino. I feel it in my bones. Forget it. I know you don't want to hear about him."

"Please," he said beckoning me back to the table. "If all I can have of you right now is coffee and talk, then talk. Go ahead and tell me about the bastard if you need to."

"I don't know how, really. I've spent so many years trying to extricate him from my mind, it feels strange to be talking like this."

"When did he contact you?" he asked.

It was an honest question. I knew what his reaction would be to hearing that I'd known about him all this time and had lied about not having seen him in so many years. My instincts told me to play it safe, but the charade exhausted me. Risk didn't mean what it used to anymore. I looked around the room. I listened to the outside drone of faint voices mixed with the buzz of streetlights and rubber tires against the road. At once, I felt myself disconnect from the coffee and Gino and the years of baggage between us and revert back to my past. I pictured myself taking an elevator down to an imaginary basement. When I stepped off the lift, I returned to the only happy day of my entire childhood. Though part of me could still see Gino fidgeting at my table and sucking down the last of the coffee, another part saw Rascal in the creaky wooden rocking chair of our summerhouse in Cape Cod, Massachusetts. Every August, we drove cross country from San Diego and stayed with my mother's parents in their house by the ocean. It was in this house that the sea embedded its alluring tangle of sounds and smells in my consciousness, and because of this I moved to Barcelona.

As Gino sat a foot in front of me waiting to hear my answer to this eternal nagging question, some part of my mind showed Rascal rocking in the creaky chair playing his guitar and singing me the old Cuban melodies that his mother sang to him. It was boiling hot that day and the car wouldn't start. When we set out on foot toward the beach, the sky turned dark and rain covered every square inch of the landscape. So we hooded our heads with beach towels and ran back to the cottage, opened all the doors and windows and sat with Rascal all afternoon, listening to his songs and wild stories. That day was the only time I recall when we had an actual conversation. He was drunk but I was too young then to understand how this affected his speech and behavior. He rocked in the chair with his guitar and I sat on a braided rug on the floor by his feet. In between verses, he'd ask me questions.

"What's Valencia going to do when she grows up to make me proud?"

I'd just laugh nervously, as I was unprepared for his questions and unaccustomed to interacting with him. Sometimes I said I would grow up to be a prima ballerina. I knew I wanted to dance even when I was eight. After the rains stopped that day, my mother took me to the little store in town to buy a toothbrush and a comb since I'd forgotten to pack them in my pink suitcase. When we got back, Rascal had cooked steaks on the grill. We ate supper outside on the wet grass under a tapestry of stars. My brother and I walked down to the beach with him after dark and put our hot feet in the ocean, and Rascal carried me back to the cottage on piggyback singing the whole way in his low, gravelly voice. That melody is forever in my ears.

Gino Malagaris was lying on the living room couch when my brain returned to the here and now. He was snoring, but only feigning sleep.

"Gino," I nudged him.

He moaned and sat up. "So you don't want to tell me after all then."

"Tell you what?"

He scowled and crossed his arms in front of him. He knew all my tricks.

"All right," I said. "Rascal sent a note to me

through a friend."

"What friend?" he asked, obviously on to me.

I put up my hands and sighed. "I send over a plate of paella and a thermos of gazpacho to his café every Sunday. Leanne from the studio drives it over there."

For several minutes he said nothing. "You pay her for this?"

"Yes. I pay her."

His jaw was clenched, but I could tell he was trying not to react.

"I've been doing this since I first moved here. I found him through a private investigator."

"You could have just walked into the local post office and perused the Wanted posters, since he's been arrested so many times."

The intent was mean-spirited but based on truth.

"Does he know it was you all this time?"

"I didn't think so until I read the letter he sent with Leanne last week. He said I use his mother's recipe for gazpacho, and he'd recognize it anywhere."

Gino got up and stood by the door. "What does he want with you?"

"He wants to give me something, he said."

"It's a trick, Valencia," he said pointing at my face. "I hope you know he's playing a game, manipulating you for his own warped amusement."

"Maybe once in your life you could stop being a damned stereotype."

"You should talk," he said, and kissed my cheek before walking away.

Three days later I called the pay phone at the Harp and Mandolin. I asked for the owner and said it was personal business. A gritty, smoker's voice answered with an abrupt hello.

"Alonso Perez?" I asked just to be sure.

There was a short pause on the other end of the phone, during which I gazed out my kitchen window at a prized view of the Collserola Hills west of town. The sun was spilling its yellow paint on the rolling landscape and lit up every bump and nuance. I could have stayed there an hour looking at the same thing.

"Who's calling?"

"It's Val," I said. Nothing more was needed.

"Valencia?" he said with a heavy squeak in his throat. "Is it you?"

"Yes. Do you want to meet me tomorrow?"

"Tell me where and when."

The next morning, I found my father, Rascal Perez, leaning against a mosaics gallery in the Gothic Quarter of Barcelona called Castaways. Fitting combination. Smoking the same brown cigarettes he'd smoked when I was a child, his eyes were following the curves of women's bodies as they walked past him. Some in shorts and huaraches, some with short skirts and high heels, and elegant silver-haired sophisticates in long black linen. Though folklore regarded him as one of Barcelona's most renowned con men, he was an ultimate sucker for women. I laughed to myself as I approached the gallery, watching his long-haired, razor stubbled head jerk left, then right, giving equal consideration to every woman that passed before him. He didn't see me until I was just about stepping on his feet.

His movements froze when he caught my eye. "I would know that face anywhere. Valencia, Valencia. Thank God you look like your mother."

I allowed myself to laugh at the sentiment, though still kept most of my heart locked up in its cast iron vault. He grabbed me and held his arms around me for several awkward minutes. I tried not to pull away. "Do you still play the mandolin?" I heard myself ask for no reason.

Rascal shook his head and smiled, showing teeth cast in gray from so many years of smoking. He was still leaning against the outside wall of the gallery. "You know that I do."

"Why do you say that?"

"You show up at the waterfront to hear the quartet every Friday night. You arrive at the same time every week and sit in exactly the same place.

You've even worn the same color pants the last few times. Do you think I don't know this? Do you think I don't nearly cry every time I taste your gazpacho? If you think just because we haven't spoken all this time that you're not a part of my life, you're not as smart as I always thought you'd be."

I stuffed my hands in my pockets and considered his monologue. He didn't speak for a while either; just puffed away on one cigarette after the other looking at girls. The front of the gallery always impressed me as being gaudy. Most of the mosaic pieces on the walls inside were smallish, neat, and conservative. But the gallery's exterior had a twenty-foot tall red and green giant fish monstrosity leaning its hideous mouth down to the front door with brightly colored tiles surrounding it, all wrapped around a thick black pole. It made me dizzy to look up at it. Rascal put his cigarettes away and motioned for me to follow him.

Well that's that, I thought. He knows that I know, and I know that he knows. It didn't mean anything, really. We'd secretly been part of each other's lives for a long time. Knowing this didn't change the dynamic of a father and daughter not speaking a word for sixteen years.

Gino seemed to sum it up nicely once. He said, "Rascal's a hardened criminal, Val. No one could ever have a normal relationship with someone like him." But I knew now that I neither wanted nor needed normalcy in my life. I taught Flamenco lessons at my own dance studio and produced marginally commercial watercolor paintings on the side. I spent most mornings cooking, hardly ever wore shoes, never shopped in the same place twice and stayed up all night planning the phases of my life. Normalcy, to me, had always been attributed to people who get up at 7:00 and go to work in a climate-controlled office and go home to a night of television. I hadn't owned a television in ten years. I washed all my clothes by hand and would have gotten cream for my coffee every morning by milking the cow out back if I had one. I was perfectly satisfied living this 19th century life, where technology played no role and the day's considerations involved long walks to the market, teaching in my studio, and staying up reading by candlelight. Of course I enjoyed the luxury of refrigeration and modern plumbing, but there were still plenty of places in Barceloneta that had neither. It was known for being a "modernized" 19th century fishing village with lots of seafood restaurants and boats docked in the harbor. I suspected Rascal liked the same things about it as I did. After all, he'd been here for thirty years.

I followed him down a dreary, smelly alley between two rows of brick buildings, nudging my body against the dirty dumpsters to avoid stepping in puddles left over from yesterday's rain. Smoke from his perpetual cigarettes drifted in my face, which in part masked the rancid smell of spoiled milk and moldy bread. We stood side by side on the edge of a main street waiting for cars to go by, then crossed to continue our alleyway pilgrimage. We entered one of the long brick buildings on the right through a large, steel, white-painted door that led to a warehouse space.

"Where are we going?" I asked him, sorrier by the minute that I ever agreed to this meeting.

"I want to give you something."

I felt restless now, my hands tingled. The temperature in the building was about ninety degrees. I wondered if we could be in the basement of the Italian bakery where I'd bought loaves of bread. Rascal walked slower now as we made our way through a labyrinth of pipes and storage containers. On the left was a wall of heavy steel drums, most likely filled with flour and sugar for baking.

We slowed our pace as we came to a main room with hanging lights and tables set up in rows of four. It looked like a caterer's kitchen after serving a party of fifty, with rolled up tablecloths on each table, splattered flour covering everything — floor, chairs, boxes stacked in one corner, and dirty plates were stacked in a huge stone sink against the back wall. Rascal stood firmly in one spot surveying the room with his eyes and senses. Like a hound, he sniffed the air and walked into an adjacent office, then another, then back to the room we'd started in.

"How's your dancing going?" he asked moving toward the steel drums we'd passed on the way through the other warehouse.

I didn't answer. My fists clenched involuntarily, but there was no sense in avoiding conversation. After all, we'd spent the last sixteen years doing that like two foolish old ladies feuding over an adolescent dispute. I'd always been intrigued by human behavior as it relates to grudges and family history. Even if the reasons are just and you were deliberately wronged, there was no avoiding the cold fact that time dilutes all feelings. Anger, resentment, hatred, even love. I watched Rascal Perez pace the floors of the warehouse wringing his hands and mumbling to himself in Cuban and tried to resurrect the same potency of my hatred for him into my heart. But all that was left of that now were a few dark shadows scattered on some hazy memories.

"Ah ha!" I heard him say from the other side of the wall. He was trying to pull away one of the heavy drums, but it wouldn't budge.

"Help me with this, Valencia. Please?"

I got on the other side and tried to pull it out from the wall, but it didn't move.

"How do you know this is the one?" I asked.

He pointed to some yellow lettering on the

side near the base of it. The steel was stamped with the word 'Mondrago.'

"What's in here?"

"Something I've been keeping for you for a long time."

"Why do you want to give it to me now?"

"I have my reasons," he said.

Some voices could be heard from the other side of the warehouse, maybe the caterers coming back downstairs to clean up their mess. While Rascal searched for a crowbar or similar tool, I sat on one of the individual drums and thought about the fish I would be catching in the morning. After a month of being without me, Gino was ten seconds away from a full-blown coronary. He had sustained the requisite amount of torture and I got my few days of solitude. So I'd agreed to go fishing in the little cove off of the harbor where we fished every day when we first met.

After thirty minutes of struggling with the drum, Rascal finally pried the lid open enough to stick his hand in. Flour landed all over him and the floor as he pulled out his arm with a box attached to it. He smiled at me and held up the box like it was a forty-pound bluefish. With tufts of flour in his hair and on his forehead, he looked just like the Rascal of my childhood — comic, unkempt, and teeming with ideas and energy. As I looked at him, I felt invisible icicles in my heart begin to melt.

"I found it. Come over here," he said moving toward the back door that had been propped open a few inches. He blew off most of the flour and wiped the rest of it off on his pant legs.

"Why was it buried in flour?"

He rolled his eyes. "It's a safe place. Don't you think?"

"Depends on what it is."

He ignored me and fumbled with the box's miniature padlock, pausing after each step to wipe his shiny brow with flour-covered fingers. He pulled out his key ring and stuck a tiny key into the opening. Finally, after a minute, it clicked. The box, lined in red velvet, contained something wrapped in sheer white lace. After another brow wipe, he removed the lace with the care of a surgeon during a heart transplant.

"Take it," he said.

Three folds of the lace, then the untying of satin ribbon and I found a gold medallion. Not a color of gold I recognized from my own jewelry collection. Could it be solid, I wondered, carefully picking it up. Its hefty weight betrayed its general age; the ornate etchings on the back showed 18th-century artistry. On the front was a large, square ruby dulled by dust and years, maybe centuries of neglect, and four brilliant blue sapphire baguettes on the top and bottom of it. The gems were sunk low into the setting, allowing the refined beauty of the gold to overtake its embellishments. I could hardly breathe for a minute. When I glanced at Rascal with my head still pointing down toward the box, I saw tears in his eyes.

"Where did you get this?" I asked in a whisper.

"My grandfather Ignacio married a Flamenco dancer from Andalusia in 1910. You were named after her. When my grandmother got older and couldn't dance any longer, Ignacio convinced her to open a dance studio to pass on some of what she'd learned in her career to young dancers wanting to learn the art form. So one day a young woman showed up at one of her beginning classes and introduced herself as Marta Luna."

Oh my God, I thought. My grandmother was Marta Luna's dance teacher? Marta Luna, the most renowned Flamenco dancer in all of Spain and the model on which all aspects of modern Flamenco were based? How could I have not known this? I glared at Rascal disapprovingly, trying to gauge how much of this story was based in reality. And though as a con artist he had little credibility for telling the truth, a part of me believed him. He was breathing heavily and kept wiping his palms on his pants. I could tell he had been waiting to tell this story for a long time.

"What does this have to do with the medallion?"

"It belonged to Marta," he said as if she'd been a personal friend. "Your grandmother was her dance teacher for almost twenty years, and in all that time she never let Marta pay for a single lesson. I suppose she showed so much promise and dedication to the art that she didn't want her to worry about mundane things like money. Marta married an archaeologist who spent his career digging up artifacts from shipwrecks."

My throat got tight and my vocal cords constrained. I could hardly pull any air through my nostrils to fill my lungs. The smell of fresh bread and cigarette smoke filtered down to us from upstairs through the vents. I felt both nauseous and elated.

"He found this medallion, the Mondrago Amulet as it was called, buried in the ocean floor thirty miles off the coast of Barcelona in 1957. Later, they discovered that it came from a shipwreck found close to Gibraltar, but at the time he was doing research on the Justina, another shipwreck. I don't remember the details of it, but he laid legal claim to it and the other artifacts he found at the same time. He sold all of them privately but kept the amulet for Marta. She loved the big red stone. Said it had some power over her that connected her to dance. When my grandmother had her knee operated on for the last time, she threatened to sell the studio. More than just a dream to her, it had been the whole reason she got up every morning. But after a difficult recovery, she said the desire to teach had left her heart and her mind. That there was no wisdom left to pass on. So Marta went to see her in the hospital and brought her this box as payment for all the years of lessons she gave her. She said in it she would find her reason to keep teaching and to keep dancing. I know you are having these same thoughts, Valencia. So now I'm giving the medallion to you."

How did he know this? Paternal instinct? After all, the only person I'd told about it was Gino.

"Because you want me to keep the studio open?"

He rubbed his chin. "So that you'll stay connected to your past. I think this medallion meant more to my grandmother than all the years she was a dance teacher. Like Marta, it had a power over her. She kept it as a reminder of who she had been and why she chose her one path in life. You own your own destiny. You always did. And no matter what happened with me and your mother I always knew you would turn out all right."

Yeah I did, no thanks to you, I thought. But no matter what I had felt about him all my life and what I was feeling now, I knew what he said about the medallion was right, because as I held it I felt a warm energy in my hands, both subtle and intense. There were no words to describe this. I felt frozen in that moment like I had temporarily disappeared from the bakery warehouse and was transported somewhere back into my family's ancient heritage. Maybe to Andalusia in the 1950's.

I found Gino this time on the rickety bench on my back porch with a pitcher of his famous margaritas. My backyard had a partial view of the hills leaning over Barcelona. When I sat down beside him he didn't even look up.

"What did he give you this time? Another black eye?" He turned to me. "Looks like you escaped that at least."

"My lineage."

"He's got a lot of nerve."

"He's not so bad," I said, hardly believing those words could come out of my mouth. I remembered, then, that the amulet was still in the pocket of my jacket.

"So what did you decide to do about your studio?"

Now that Rascal had given me a piece of my heritage, the fate of my dance studio seemed altogether small. A week ago, I was fatherless with a husband I couldn't be with any longer. But now, the capacity of my heart to feel and love seemed infinite. Gino looked at me the way he had looked at me years ago, like I was his beautiful Flamenco princess. All the years of broken promises and disappointment, of distance and longing, that had passed between us since then were masked by an unspeakable power in his eyes. Not as volatile as passion or as restless as infatuation, it was more like friendship. The deepest and rarest of all friendship. The kind that's transformed over time out of chemistry and nature, and only found on the other side of pain. In his frozen expression was a gesture of acceptance. I knew he would learn to live with whatever decision I made. Stay or quit. Teach or retire. To him, I would still be long-haired Valencia Perez, the Flamenco dancer, who borrowed a bag of sugar from him once.

Without answering, I let the distant Collserola Hills hold my gaze while I sparked an image of a young, long-legged gawky girl knocking on the door of my studio.

I Remember

by Michael Nelson

I am an old man now, and as such I am ensconced in the soft chair in the corner, while the festivities of Christmas unfold all around me. Their attention is occupied with the excitement of the moment defined by bright wrapping paper and the anticipation of what's next. My wistful eyes watch as they shout and wriggle out their energy. For me there are more Christmases behind me than ahead, and I am an afterthought of the present one. Comfortably in the corner, present but only as wallpaper, and I remember as I watch, I remember;

I remember the joy of running breathlessly because I could

I remember that blush when she made eye contact for the first time

I remember the infectious laughter of my infant sons

I remember your beckoning eyes in the darkened bedroom

I remember the first time I saw you as you stood in your nightshirt before the sun bright window.

I remember my first handshake, when it meant something

I remember cool baths on summer afternoon when it was too hot to play outside anymore.

I remember the icy cold water of swimming in the stock tank.

I remember the criminal intent of my sisters who were smarter than I was, and their clever plots.

I remember the smell of fresh hay, and the bump of the hay wagon over a rough ground

I remember the pain of remorse when I disappointed myself.

I remember my first breathless kiss, and the taste of the breath mint on her lips.

I remember the heart melting moment of the first time I gazed into my child's eyes.

I remember the terror of the bullets and tracers in the night and watching my friend die.

I remember the softness of an expensive towel.

I remember the deafening experience of a hard rock concert.

I remember children laughing in the rain and old men laughing as they watched from the porch

I remember my most memorial bowel movement

I remember my first orgasm, and the Catholic

guilt that followed because I was alone.

I remember how sweet and tender is love

I remember the shadow of despair when I was unloved and deserved to be.

I remember

I remember as they scramble in pursuit through the discarded wrapping paper, ensconced in the chair in the corner.

But I remember.

Thank you for taking the time to read this collection from the authors of Indies United Publishing House. We hope you enjoyed it and would like to encourage you to take a moment to review this collection on your favorite reading platform.

A little about Indies United

Here at Indies United, we are a co-op of like-minded authors working together to showcase our books and highlight our diversity as writers. We openly encourage and support both new and established authors in their pursuit of finding their audience while bringing to you books worth reading. Our goal is to give authors a home to call their own, while bringing fresh, innovative, and exciting books to readers all over the world.

If you are an author, please check us out at www.indiesunited.net

If you would like to connect to Indies United you can find us at:

Facebook
https://www.facebook.com/IndiesUnitedPublishin
g
OR @IndiesUnitedPublishing

Twitter
https://twitter.com/IndiesUnitedPub
OR @IndiesUnitedPub

Instagram
https://www.instagram.com/lisaorbanauthor/

Linkedin
www.linkedin.com/in/indies-united-publishing-
house

Pinterest
https://www.pinterest.com/indiesunited/

GoodReads
https://www.goodreads.com/user/show/122472367
-indies-united